MW01138502

Wednesday, June 16, 1954

Construction on the new twenty-story building for Consolidated Security at the corner of Market and Montgomery is ahead of schedule, thanks to Henry and Pam. Nick is looking forward to his office on the nineteenth floor. The twentieth floor is designed to be a restaurant. He's hoping for French or Italian. Carter wants something with less garlic.

But then an unknown man falls from the top of the steel skeleton and things grind to a halt.

When Henry gets a late-night call warning him and Nick to not investigate, Mike takes action to protect them both but Nick gets a late-night visit from some wiseguys and it doesn't end well... For them.

That's just the beginning of a tale of mobsters, refugees, and The Old Poodle Dog that twists and turns its way to a thrilling conclusion.

The Mangled Mobster

Nick Williams Mysteries

The Unexpected Heiress

The Amorous Attorney

The Sartorial Senator

The Laconic Lumberjack

The Perplexed Pumpkin

The Savage Son

The Mangled Mobster

Nick & Carter Stories

An Enchanted Beginning

The Mangled Mobster

A Nick Williams Mystery

By Frank W. Butterfield

Published With Delight

By The Author

MMXVII

The Mangled Mobster

ISBN-10: 154274623X
ISBN-13: 978-1542746236

First publication: January 2017

Be the first to know about new releases:

nickwilliamspi.com

NW07-B-20170124

Contents

For Michael & Billy

I'm sure that one of you told me
about the Old Poodle Dog long ago...

Mangled

\ˈmaŋ-gəld\

1. Injured with deep disfiguring wounds by cutting, tearing, or crushing.

Mobster

\ˈmäb-stər\

1. A member of a criminal gang.

Merriam-Webster.com. 2016.
http://www.merriam-webster.com
(31 December 2016).

Chapter 1

The Palace Hotel
San Francisco, Cal.
Wednesday, June 16, 1954
Just before 10 in the morning

I pulled the Buick up in front of The Palace Hotel on New Montgomery Street. An older man, dressed in a red uniform, walked around and opened the door.

"Welcome to The Palace, sir. Are you checking in?"

"No. I'm only going to be here for an hour or so." I added, "For a meeting. Can you keep the car close by?" I pushed a folded ten into the man's gloved hand.

Without more than glancing at the bill, he tipped his hat, smiled politely, and replied, "My pleasure. It will be right here when you're ready to depart."

"Thanks," I said. "Keys are in the ignition." I quickly walked up the steps and into the hotel.

. . .

The Palace had a storied past. The great Caruso had performed Carmen the night before the earthquake of '06 and was jolted awake when the shaking started at 5 that morning. He was so outraged at the experience that he vowed to never return to San Francisco. And he never did.

The original Palace had survived the earthquake but was destroyed during the fire that followed. The current building had opened in '09 and it was a grand dame.

President Harding was once a guest. He died in his suite on the eighth floor back in '23 and under mysterious circumstances. There was a wiseacre at school who liked to say, "He didn't make it out alive." That really busted us kids up, every time, but the history teacher was never amused.

As I walked through the magnificent lobby and outside to the Market Street side of the building, I thought about my husband, Carter Jones, an ex-fireman and the love of my life. His captain at Station 3 used to start off meetings by saying, "Back in '06, it wasn't the earthquake, boys, it was the fire, so listen up..."

The doorman courteously opened the door for me and I walked out into the bustle of Market Street. The sidewalks were jammed with men and women on their way to who knew where. The street was crowded with cars and trucks trying to move around the streetcars. There was talk of building a subway under Market Street that would move the streetcars onto tracks underground. It sure would be faster for everyone concerned but it was hard to imagine the scene in front of me without the clanging bells of the streetcars.

"Hi, Nick."

My reverie was broken by Henry Winters, Carter's best friend, former lover, and someone he'd known since childhood. They'd moved to San Francisco together in '39 by driving cross country when that wasn't an easy thing to do. Carter claimed we looked alike but Henry had green eyes compared to my brown ones and he was easily more handsome. Besides, he had a scar that ran along the right side of his face. It was a parting gift from a German officer and accentuated his good looks.

We shook hands. He looked across the street and said, "The skeleton is almost finished. With any luck, we'll start installing the windows in two weeks."

We were both looking at the frame of a twenty-story office building that stood at the corner of Market and Montgomery. We hadn't come up with a name for it yet, so it was called 600 Market Street because that was the official address given the building by the post office. It was going to be a modern square glass tower on the triangular spit of land that was bordered by Market, Montgomery, and Post.

I had bought the land in November of the year before and asked Henry, an engineer, to manage the project of getting it built. Things were moving along quickly and we hoped to be done and moved in by the end of the year.

I held onto my hat as I craned my neck and looked up at the top. There was an American flag attached to the top of the building. All forty-eight stars were fluttering in the morning breeze. It was more of a thrill to see the building so far underway than I thought it would be. And the idea of having an office up on the nineteenth floor was exciting on top of that.

Consolidated Security, the private investigation and security firm I owned, would be using floors fifteen through nineteen. The twentieth floor was designed to be a restaurant. I was hoping for French or Italian.

Carter wanted something with less garlic.

I asked, "Any new tenants?"

Henry replied, "I think so. But you have to ask Robert. He's handling all of that and I don't have time to keep track."

I nodded. Besides being Henry's squeeze, Robert Evans was my whiz-bang real estate manager. He took care of everything to do with the properties I owned, including leasing out the two airplanes I'd bought in the last year. One was a silver Lockheed Super Constellation, called *The Laconic Lumberjack* after a friend in Georgia. The other was a tan DC-7 that didn't have a name yet. Both were being used right now by some Hollywood muckety-mucks who were paying a reasonable rate for two captains, a stewardess, and the luxury of their own plane. But, I didn't keep track of who leased them and where they went any more than I tried to keep on top of who was a tenant in any of my buildings. In Robert's capable hands, my real estate business was going gangbusters.

We stood on the street for a moment more. I asked, "Wanna get some coffee?"

Henry looked at his watch. "Sure. I have about twenty minutes before I need to get back across the street."

I nodded and said, "I'm buying," as we walked back into the hotel.

. . .

The Pied Piper was the bar inside the hotel. I always felt more comfortable there than in the more famous and much larger Garden Court. Its name came from the Maxfield Parrish mural over the bar that depicted the Pied Piper of Hamlin in bright colors. The big chairs were covered in a pine green leather. The wood-paneled walls were stained a chestnut color. Like the Garden Court, the room was partially illuminated by a modest stained-glass skylight. Unlike the Garden Court, under its intricately-designed skylight and tables set among ostentatious planted palms, the Pied Piper was quiet and more like the kind of bar you'd find in the Pacific Union Club up on Nob Hill. Since it was the middle of the morning, the place was mostly empty, with one or two late risers drinking coffee and reading their newspaper.

Once we were seated and had ordered coffee, I asked Henry, "How are things between you and Robert?" The two had started going together back in November.

Henry's face brightened and he smiled. His green eyes twinkled as he said, "Good. I'm in love." He leaned in. "I'm even thinking of buying a house."

I smiled. "Where?"

"Not sure, yet. Maybe Eureka Valley. I'm ready to move out of the Tenderloin for good."

"Robert going with you?"

Right then, the waiter brought us our coffee. Henry poured some cream into his while I dropped two sugar cubes into mine. He contemplated his coffee cup for a moment. Finally, he looked up at me and said, "I hope he will." As he took a sip from his cup, I wondered what he wasn't saying. After a couple of beats, he said, "I want to tell you something, but I'm not sure how to say it."

"Just spill it. You can say anything to me, Henry." I really did love him. He was like the brother I never had. People on the street often asked if we were twins.

He smiled wanly. "Promise you won't get mad if I tell you?"

"Sure."

"It's just that..." He took another sip of his coffee. I

5

had no idea why he was stalling, but I could wait. I was good at waiting for people to say what what they needed to say.

Finally, he said, "I'm really in love."

I nodded. "Yeah."

"I mean it. I..." He stared out across the empty room. "I... This..." He took another sip. I nodded.

"Well, Nick. It's like this. I love Robert more than Carter."

I laughed quietly.

"What?" he asked.

I shrugged. "Carter was your first love. And you were his. Of course, this is different."

"But, I've known Carter most of my life. I still love him--"

"Like I love you. As a brother."

Henry seemed to relax. "Yes. As a brother."

"Look, Henry. I couldn't be more happy for you than I am right now." I leaned in a bit. "I think this is great. You've been miserable for too long. And now you have a great guy. And you're both great together." I smiled and said, "Buy a house and move in together and be happy."

Henry looked at me as though I had said the magic words. "Thanks, Nick. I will."

. . .

Henry looked at his watch. "I need to get back." We both stood up as I dropped a five on the table and began to walk to the front of the room when a voice called out, "Paging Henry Winters."

A kid in a red uniform and a square cap was standing at the door of the bar. Henry raised his hand in response. The kid nodded and waited as walked over to him.

6

"I'm Henry Winters."

"You have a message Mr. Winters. You're needed back at the site urgently."

Henry looked at me. I shrugged.

"Was there anything else in the message?"

"No, sir. But I'm told it's very urgent."

Henry gave the kid a buck. I followed him as he quickly trotted to the door and out onto Market Street.

I could see two patrol cars parked along Market in front of the building. Dodging traffic, we quickly crossed the street and made our way to the construction entrance.

A policeman was standing in front of the gate waving off onlookers. As we approached, he said, "Sorry, sir. This is a crime scene."

Henry said, "My name is Winters. I'm the project manager." Pointing at me, he said, "This is the owner of the building."

The cop stepped back and said, "Go on through."

We raced down to a spot where several people, including two cops and a police lieutenant were gathered. Pam Spaulding, the site manager working for Henry, was holding her hardhat. She looked shocked and angry.

As we walked up, I could hear the lieutenant asking, "What about safety equipment?"

Pam was indignant. "Every man up there is tied off. But, you're not listening to me. This man isn't on the construction crew. I don't know who he is."

Henry walked up to Pam while I held back. "What happened, Pam?"

She turned on him and said, "I don't have a fucking clue other than this Joe fell from the twentieth floor. I don't know who he is. Do you?"

"Pardon me, sir." That was the lieutenant. "Who are

7

you?"

Henry was looking down at the man on the ground. He turned and looked at me with an expression I didn't understand. Turning back to the lieutenant, he said, "My name is Henry Winters. I'm the project manager for this building site."

The lieutenant scribbled something on his notepad. He looked over in my direction and seemed to recognize me. He smirked and made another scribble.

I walked over and looked down at the man on the ground. He was somewhere around 40 and mostly bald. His empty eyes were looking at the sky. His arms and legs were pointed in all sorts of wrong directions. They were obviously broken. I noticed there were some red marks on his neck and that his tongue, almost blue, was hanging out of his mouth. He was dressed in a dark navy coat with trousers that matched. His red tie was undone, which I thought was interesting. He was also missing his left shoe.

I stood up and asked the lieutenant, "And you are?"

The man replied, "Lieutenant Greg Holland."

"Central Station?"

He nodded and made more notes. "So none of you recognize this man?"

I looked at the other men who were gathered around. I guessed they were all employees of Universal Construction, the firm that Pam and Henry had hired. All of them were shaking their heads.

. . .

Once the body had been removed, the lieutenant pulled Henry, Pam, and me into the temporary construction office which was cramped and only had enough room for two small desks.

Standing with his back to the door, Lieutenant

Holland took a good look at each of us. He was right at six feet. His nose was broken and had the tell-tale red lines that indicated a heavy drinker. He had brown eyes and brown hair and reminded me of Andy Anderson, one of the guys at the office, in that he was handsome in a nondescript way. A casual onlooker would have trouble remembering any of his facial traits other than his broken nose. He was wearing a London Fog coat over a brown suit with a blue tie that was loose at the neck.

He asked, "Are you sure none of you know who that man is?"

I nodded and watched Henry and Pam. Henry seemed to know something but said, "I have no idea." Pam, who was still angry, said the same thing.

I looked at the lieutenant. "Do you know who he is?"

The lieutenant shrugged and changed the subject. "We've done as much as we can here. You're free to resume work." He put his notebook into his pocket, opened the door, walked down the steps, and was gone.

I asked Pam, "Do you want to go back to work?" It wasn't my question to ask but Henry seemed to be lost in thought.

She said, "Hell, yes. We're coming in ahead of schedule and I don't want that fucked up."

I smiled and said, "Well, don't let me stop you."

Henry didn't say anything. After a moment, Pam banged open the door, cussing under her breath, and was gone.

"Henry?"

He was looking at the floor. At the sound of my voice, he looked surprised to hear his name. "Yes?"

"Who was that man?"

"What man?"

I rolled my eyes. "The one who was strangled and

dumped off the twentieth floor."

"Strangled?" Henry was still looking at the floor. He leaned against one of the desks and sighed.

"Yes. Those were rope burns on his neck. Who was he?"

"Johnny Russell. Riatti Supply. Concrete." Saying the words seemed painful. And it was understandable. Riatti was known to be operated by the local mob family, run by Michael Abati.

"Why didn't you tell the lieutenant?"

Henry shrugged. "I was embarrassed, I guess."

"Why?"

Henry looked up. His green eyes were worried. "He was here to collect his payoff."

I wasn't surprised that it was happening. But I was surprised to be hearing about it right at that moment and not earlier.

"How much?"

"Five thousand."

"Where was that kinda money supposed to come from?"

"A thousand from me and the rest from Universal."

I grabbed Henry by the shoulders and shook him. "What the fuck, Henry?"

This got his attention. "What?"

"Why are you only now telling me about this? You shouldn't have to pay any of it. That's my problem, not yours."

I let go of him. He looked down again. "That's how Mr. Bechtel handles it."

I laughed. "When your company gets to be the size of Bechtel, then you can handle it like that. You know a thousand bucks is nothing for me." I opened my wallet and pulled out ten hundreds.

He shook his head. "I was supposed to pay him after

10

seeing you."

I put the cash back in my wallet. "So, do you have the whole stash that you were supposed to give this guy?"

Henry nodded. He took out a set of keys and walked over to a filing cabinet. The bottom drawer had a kind of modified padlock on the outside. Leaning over, he unlocked the drawer and pulled it open. He reached in and brought out a thick envelope. "Universal sent this over by messenger early this morning."

I asked, "Did you count it?"

Henry closed the drawer and stood up. "No."

"Did you even open it?"

He looked at me. "No. Why?"

"How do you know there's four grand in there?"

Henry shrugged. I laughed. "Son, you gotta learn how to be in the construction business. Always check. Always."

He handed me the envelope which was sealed with cellophane tape. I grabbed a pair of scissors off the desk and slit open the envelope. When I looked inside, I found a stack of newsprint cut to look like currency. I held out the envelope and said, "See?"

Henry sat down abruptly in the desk chair and put his head in his hands. I sat on the edge of the desk and said, "Rookie mistake. Don't sweat it."

Henry looked up, his face a picture of misery and moaned, "They didn't cover any of this when I was in school at Cal."

I laughed and said, "Buck up, cowboy. We need to go pay your friends over at Universal a visit. And we need to get there before the cops do." That reminded me of something. "Can I use the phone?" I asked.

Henry nodded glumly. "Sure."

I reached over, picked up the receiver, and dialed the office.

"Consolidated Security." It was Marnie, my gem of a secretary.

"Lemme talk to Mike."

"He ain't here, Nick. He's over at the North Station."

"The minute he gets back or, if he calls in, give him this message. Ready?"

"Shoot."

"Lieutenant Holland. Central Station. Unknown guy pushed off twentieth floor of 600 Market today around 10:15 or so. There's more, but I wanna tell him in person and after he's checked in with Holland. Got that?"

"Sure. Gruesome, huh?"

"Like a goddam pretzel."

"Gee, Nick."

"I know. Thanks, doll." I put down the phone and stood up. "Come on cowboy. Put on your hat and let's get saddled up. We have some cattle rustlers to chase down."

Henry smiled briefly, put on his hat, and we made our way through the construction site and out onto Market Street.

Chapter 2

The Shell Building
100 Bush Street
Wednesday, June 16, 1954
A few minutes before noon

Henry and I walked into the ornate lobby of The Shell Building through the main entrance. As we were waiting at the elevator, he said, "This building is beautiful."

I nodded. "But I like the modern look of our building better."

Henry smiled and said, "Yes. I think it's going to really stand out against the skyline." He looked around. "Is Jeffery's office still here?"

I nodded and gave him a tight smile. Jeffery Klein, Esquire, had been my lover, my friend, and my lawyer. Now he was none of those.

Back in '43, I'd inherited a large trust from my Great-Uncle Paul on my twenty-first birthday. I was in the

Navy at the time and met Jeffery through the commander of the ship I was serving on. Once I was back home, we'd become lovers. He'd successfully helped me when my entire family had sued to have the inheritance voided. Our relationship was winding down about the time I met Carter in '47 but we stayed friends until the previous summer when Jeffery had decided to get out of the life and get married to a nice girl by the name of Rachel. In a synagogue. By a rabbi. The last I'd heard, Rachel was expecting. That was nice.

The elevator doors opened. There wasn't a doorman like there had been the last time I'd been in the building. Instead, there was a bright and shiny panel of buttons. Henry pressed the number seven and the doors began to close.

Just as they did, I heard a familiar voice say, "Hold that, please!" I put my hand in the middle and forced the doors back open.

"Hi, Nick. Henry." It was Jeffery Klein, Esquire, himself.

Henry nodded but said nothing as Jeffery walked in. I said, "How are you?"

"Good. Rachel's expecting a baby."

"When?" I asked.

"November."

"Congratulations." I tried to insert some enthusiasm in my voice, but it didn't take.

"Thanks."

After a long moment, the car stopped on the seventh floor. Jeffery asked, "Universal?"

I said, "Yeah."

"They're bad news, Nick."

I lifted my hat to Jeffery and followed Henry out into the hallway. The doors closed silently behind us and he was gone.

"How much weight do you think he's gained?" asked Henry as we walked down the long hallway.

"Does it matter?" was my growling reply.

Henry said, "Sorry."

"He's getting fat because he's unhappy and not getting any on the side. But let's don't dance on his grave."

Henry said, "Sure, Nick. Sorry about that."

I stopped walking and grabbed Henry's arm. The hallway was deserted and the door to Universal's office was made of frosted glass. I pulled Henry into a hug, which pushed both our hats back but not off, and kissed him on the lips. I held him close and whispered in his ear, "Stop fretting, cowboy. We're gonna get this all cleared up." As I released him, I said, "You let me do all the talking. Got that?"

Henry looked at me. "You always know how to make me feel better, Nick."

I smiled and said, "It's the kiss. That's what does it."

Henry smiled at me and kissed me on the cheek in reply.

. . .

"I don't know what you think this is, but I don't take kindly to shake-downs."

We were standing in the office of Thomas Rutledge, President of Universal Construction, Incorporated. His office was in the same location as Jeffery's, whose was three stories up, and he had the same view of the bay. The Golden Gate Bridge was on the left. The Ferry Building was on the right. And Alcatraz was in between. Above it all was a big blue sky.

I said, "This ain't a shake-down, Mr. Rutledge. What I wanna know is why you sent over forty pieces of newsprint instead of four thousand dollars?"

15

"What are you talking about?" Rutledge was about 6'2" tall. He was somewhere north of fifty. His hair was gray and cut short. He was a big man but he was fit. He was standing up, leaning on his desk, and looked like he was ready for a fight.

"Didn't you order the concrete for my building?"

"Your building? Who are you?"

"Nicholas Williams. You're working through Henry here to build my office building at 600 Market Street. You better get your story straight because a man was strangled and then pushed off the top of that building this morning at 10:15. The cops are gonna be paying you a visit pretty soon."

This got through to him. He sighed deeply and sat down in his chair. It was of the big leather type and looked like butterscotch.

"Damn."

"What?" I asked.

He didn't answer. Instead, he pressed down on a button and barked, "Get Keller in here, now!"

"Yes, sir," replied the voice of the dragon lady who guarded the inner sanctum. We'd had a hell of a time getting in.

Running his hand over his hair, Rutledge smiled. "Gentlemen. Please. Have a seat."

We both did just that.

"Now. Let's start over. Mr. Williams, it's a pleasure to finally meet you." He pointedly did not smile nor did he offer his hand. As my notoriety spread, I was becoming used to this.

"And, yes. We bid on the job advertised by Mr. Winters. And we're happy to be working on it. I hear we're coming in ahead of schedule."

I didn't say, "Because your crew is being managed by a girl," even though I wanted to. I figured I'd save that line for later.

"And, yes, I know that in San Francisco, like so many cities across America, there are hidden and unexpected costs in construction. And, in San Francisco, that particularly applies to concrete."

Right then, a side door opened and the oiliest man I'd ever seen oozed in the office. He was about 5'9", thin as a rail, had dark hair slicked back to a shine, and was all smiles. He should have had the word, "snake," tattooed across his forehead.

"May I introduce you to one of my managers? This is Vernon Keller."

Keller walked over and offered his hand to me which I shook. I wanted to run my handkerchief over my palm afterward, but I didn't.

"Vernon, this is Mr. Nicholas Williams. He's the owner at 600 Market Street. Of course, you know Mr. Winters already."

Mr. Keller nodded coolly. He said, "I didn't know Mr. Williams was the owner. Henry, you never mentioned that."

I stood up and said, "Why does that matter?"

"Well, Mr. Williams, it's always a good idea to know who the players are in any project."

I tried not to roll my eyes. Before I could speak, Mr. Rutledge said, "There was a tragic accident at the site today, Vernon. Seems that a man was strangled and then thrown from the twentieth floor. Do you know anything about that?"

I watched the thin man's eyes dart around the room. He was obviously trying to decide on how to answer the question. After a quick moment, he said, "Sure, Mr. Rutledge. I just got a call from the site. Terrible news. And no one knew who he was."

Henry stood up. "You know exactly who he was."

Mr. Keller leaned back on his heels and asked, "Who?"

"Your contact at Riatti Supply."

Forming his mouth into the shape of an "O," Mr. Keller said, "Really? Johnny Russell?"

Henry nodded. I asked, "And, I'm wondering why, when you sent over the money for the 'unexpected cost,' as your boss put it, you sent Henry a stack of newsprint."

Now Keller looked trapped but he maintained his posture. "I don't know what you mean."

I pulled the envelope out of my coat and showed it to him, without handing it over. Rutledge came around to look at it. "This is what I mean. Delivered by messenger this morning. This was supposed to be the four thousand dollar payoff. Henry was chipping in a thousand from his own pocket." I put the envelope back in my pocket.

Rutledge looked at Keller and said, "I thought the total was three thousand. That's how much I signed for yesterday."

Keller licked his lips and smiled. "That's right, Mr. Rutledge. I put in a thousand of my own. I only felt it was fair." This was such unmitigated bullshit that it was all I could do to keep from laughing.

I looked at Henry and tilted my head. He nodded. I said, "Well, we'll leave you two so you have time to get your story straight before the cops get here. Keller, I hope you have witnesses for where you were at 10:15 this morning."

With that, I walked to the big double doors we'd entered through. After Henry went through, I turned and said, "Oh, and Rutledge?"

The big man turned and looked at me. "Yes, Mr. Williams?"

"Your boys are doing a great job and they're coming in ahead of schedule. Please thank 'em for me."

He smiled and nodded. "I certainly will."

I pointed at Keller and said, "But, it's not because of this lying piece of shit." Keller's eyes widened in outrage. "It's because Henry hired a girl to do the site management."

. . .

Once we were down in the lobby, I said, "Lemme call in." Henry nodded. I walked over to the row of phone booths, entered one, and closed the door. I dropped in a dime and dialed the office. This time Robert answered.

"Mike there?" I asked.

"Not yet. But he called in and Marnie told me to tell you that she delivered the message."

"Good." I paused, trying to decide whether to say the next part. Taking a chance, I said, "Robert, I need to tell you something but you didn't hear it from me."

"Sure, Nick. What is it?"

"Henry's had a tough day."

"I figured. Such a tragedy."

"It's more than that. I can't go into the details but I just wanted to let you know he's gonna need some extra T.L.C."

Robert sighed. "Thanks, Nick. I'll be real sweet to him."

I smiled to myself. "You do that. And, thanks, kid. But, remember. You didn't hear it from me."

"I'll remember."

Chapter 3

Offices of Consolidated Security
777 Bush Street, Third Floor
Wednesday, June 16, 1954
Around 5 in the afternoon

Mike Robertson, President of Consolidated Security, my best friend and first lover, and a former police lieutenant at the North Station was sitting across from me and next to another one of our guys, Ben White. Ben had once been a police officer at the Central Station. They both lost their jobs thanks to the fact that I'd confronted George Hearst a year earlier and they were known to be friendly with me. The same had happened to my husband, Carter, and Ben's squeeze, Carlo Martinelli. It still rankled, but I was doing my best to make it up to these guys.

Carter and Martinelli were gone for an overnight trip to Santa Paula, down south. They were helping a small fire department investigate a possible arson. They were due back the next day and, since I hated sleeping alone, I was already looking forward to seeing them walk through the door.

Meanwhile, I'd asked Mike and Ben to go over what we knew about the events at the construction site earlier in the day.

"So, waddaya know about this Holland?" I asked.

Mike looked at Ben and said, "I never worked with the guy. What about you?"

Ben nodded. "Straight shooter. Goes by the book. I once saw him break up an interrogation that was going too hard. Good guy. But," and he shook his head, "no friend of ours."

By that, I knew Ben meant that Holland wouldn't like working with or being around a bunch of queers. I nodded and asked Mike, "You talk to him, yet?"

He shook his head. "Nope. Left a message and haven't heard back. He may not be interested in talking to me."

I sighed. We tried to work with the City police and fire departments. But they were under a lot of political pressure to steer clear of us. The smaller towns and villages in California were happy to hire us to come in and help when they needed it. We had reasonable rates and were usually available right when they wanted us. It seemed like we were only notorious in San Francisco, itself. It didn't matter much. We had more than enough business and Mike was hiring at least one new man per month.

The story for these new guys was always the same. Somehow the truth that they were in the life would be discovered and they would be fired. We were happy to have most of them if they wanted to work for us.

In fact, Carter and Martinelli were working with a new hire. He was a former fireman and was, in fact, living with Mike. His name was Ray Hunter. He'd been married and, in the divorce, it came out about his proclivities and that was the end of his work as a San Francisco fireman. According to Carter, who was his boss, he was working out just fine.

I asked Mike, "What do you know about Universal?"

"Probably the same as you. Used to be connected to the mob. A few years ago, they sold out to a former Yale football star. Comes from the east coast. Guy by the name of Rutledge. He's been trying to clean the place up."

I nodded. "I heard it was because the Army had hired them to work at the Presidio and their mob connections were made public."

Mike nodded.

"I also heard that this Rutledge was somehow politically connected."

Mike said, "Yeah. His father was a Republican bigwig in Connecticut. I don't know all the details, but there's some link between the son coming in to take over the company and the father's pals. I think it has to do with the Army. But I'm not sure."

"He tried to pretend he didn't know about the payoff, at first. Then he does a song and a dance about 'unexpected costs.' But, I think he's more on the up-and-up than that weasel Keller."

Ben asked, "You said his name was Vernon Keller?"

I nodded. "You heard of him?"

Ben closed his eyes for a moment. "I have. I just can't remember where."

I laughed. "Bunco Squad?"

Ben shook his head. "No. It was something else."

"Well, he tried to pull a grift on his employer. That newsprint scam is as old as Moses. I didn't think anyone tried shit like that anymore."

Mike laughed and said, "It's tried and true." He

stopped and thought for a moment. "Poor Henry."

I nodded. "Yeah. I told Robert to take off early so he could get ready to deal with the incoming wounded. Henry had a rough day today." I sighed. "And we saw Jeffery."

Mike cocked his head to the side, "And?"

"He's put on a few pounds. That just means he isn't getting any sex. I know that much."

"Rachel's pregnant?" Mike asked.

"Yes."

Ben, not knowing he was walking into a landmine, smirked at me and asked, "Then who's the father?"

I couldn't help myself. "Jeffery is, you little shit. Who do you think?"

Mike sat up and said, "Easy there, Nick."

I took a deep breath and said, "Sorry about that, Ben. Thing is, as angry as I am about Jeffery, I just can't stand it when someone else picks on him. He thinks he's between a rock and a hard place." I looked down at my desk and started moving things around. "Hell. You know. You were there. He had a real bad time last summer in Mexico."

Ben nodded soberly. "You're right, Nick. I shouldn't have said that. I'm sorry."

I stood up. "It's alright, kid." To change the subject, I said, "Well, we're all fireman widows tonight. What are you two up to?"

Ben stood up. "I'm going to see a movie with a friend. Then we're going to the Tonga Room at the Fairmont."

I smiled. "Sounds good."

Ben pursed his lips. "It's OK. I don't like sleeping alone."

I walked over and slapped him on the back. "Me, neither, kid. Me, neither."

He said, "Unless you need me, I'll be heading out

then."

I smiled and said, "Thanks for your help, Ben. Sorry about what I said earlier."

Mike stood up and said, "Meet me here at 9 in the morning. I have a job for you."

Ben nodded, turned, and walked out the front door.

Once he was gone, Mike crossed his arms, looked at me, and said, "What gives, Nick?" He was a big man. He stood 6'5" and had what I liked to call a monster handsome face. He had jet black hair, a heavy forehead, and intensely piercing blue eyes. When he was happy, he was surprisingly attractive. When he was upset, I always thought of the villagers fleeing the monster. This was one of those times.

"Jeffery?" I asked.

"Yeah. I thought that was over and you were done."

I nodded and sighed. "It is and I am. But, seeing him today..." I thought for a moment. "He looked so sad. There's no other way to put it."

. . .

Somehow, Mike convinced me to go with him to Gene Compton's Cafeteria at South Van Ness and Market for dinner. We walked in, got our trays of food, paid, and sat down in the dining room. I hadn't been to the place in a few years. Looking around, I didn't see any familiar faces. We took a table in the corner so we could watch and see if anyone we knew wandered in. It was just past 7 and that was early for the old crowd. The sun was still in the sky, for one thing. Most of the old gang usually only came out at night.

I had my old favorite: navy bean soup and a turkey sandwich. It tasted just as good as I remembered. Mike had the daily special: ham steak, potatoes au gratin, green beans, and a pineapple upside-down cake. We both drank coffee.

"When was the last time you were here?" That was Mike. In between bites of ham.

"Had to be '50, at the latest. I stopped coming once Mack died." Mack McKnight had been a close friend. We'd been lovers on the ship that brought us back stateside after the war. We'd become close friends once we were back in San Francisco. He'd re-enlisted when things heated up in Korea and died when his ship hit a landmine.

"So, how are things with you and Ray?" I asked.

Mike shrugged. "Good. I guess." He took a bite of ham.

As I took a sip of my coffee, I looked at him.

"What gives?"

Mike swallowed and wiped his mouth. "I dunno. I'm sure it's nothing. Just seems like he's not as interested as he was."

"How long has it been?"

"Six months."

I nodded. This was not going well. "Wanna talk about it?" I asked.

He shook his head and had another bite of ham. I could feel a melancholy settle over me. I didn't know if it was the memory of Mack, the obvious end of Mike's relationship, or something else.

I looked up to see Mike's striking blue eyes piercing me. He asked, "How about you and Carter?"

I moved my spoon around in the soup bowl. "Good."

"What's wrong, Nick?"

"Who said anything was wrong?"

"Your face. You look unhappy."

I sighed. The truth was more complicated than that. On the previous Christmas day, I'd learned what really happened to my mother and why she had abruptly left my sister and me back in '29. That was also the day my father announced his plan to marry Leticia Wilson, the mother of my secretary, Marnie. She was a woman I adored and was also a little afraid of. Their wedding in April almost didn't happen but then it did and the two lovebirds had spent a month in Europe on their honeymoon.

The biggest question of my life had been answered. I'd reconciled with my father who'd been a bastard most of my life and who was now like a purring cat living the high life in his big house on Sacramento Street. Marnie was dating a nice man from San Mateo and it was looking like they might be getting married at some point. Business was never better. I was making more money than anyone, including myself, could believe. Life should have been wonderful. But, it wasn't.

I reached into my coat pocket and pulled out a package of Camels and my old beat-up Zippo lighter. I offered one to Mike, who took it. After I lit his cigarette, I lit my own, and leaned back while I took in a big drag. That always made me feel a little more relaxed. As I exhaled to the side, I took another sip of coffee.

Mike put his elbows on the table, held the cigarette between his big hands, and looked at me.

After a moment of this, I said, "I know that technique, Mike."

He took another drag off the Camel and just smiled at me. Finally, he asked, "Well?"

Taking another puff, I breathed out and said, "I should be happy but I ain't. I don't know what else to say." I stubbed out my cigarette in the ashtray on the table and stood up.

I wanted out of this place. It was like a tomb. There were too many bad memories. I felt like I was in a swirl.

I could almost hear Mack, as if he was at a nearby table laughing and talking. I wanted out. But I just stood there and stared off in the distance.

Mike stood up and said, "Gimme your keys."

"What?"

"Gimme your keys. I don't know what's happening inside of you but it looks like it's all about to come out. Come on." He reached out his hand. "Hand 'em over."

Without thinking much more about it, I pulled my keys out of my pocket and gave them to Mike.

. . .

By the time Mike pulled the Buick into the driveway, I was shivering. I wasn't sick. I wasn't even cold. But I was shivering.

We walked up the steps and he unlocked the door. I followed him inside and pulled the door closed behind me. I followed his lead, as if I couldn't seem to think for myself, and put my hat on the rack in the hallway.

He said, "Sit down, Nick." So, leaving on my coat, I sat down on the sofa in the sitting room. I watched him walk over to the little bar by the phone alcove and build a couple of drinks. When he was done, he walked over to where I was sitting. He handed my a glass with a double shot of whiskey and said, "Drink." So, I did.

I could feel the warm liquid going down my throat and into my belly. It felt good. I watched as Mike stood in front of me. He took off his coat, dropped it on a chair, and loosened his tie. He sat down right next to me, squeezing in tight. He reached around me, took the empty glass out of my hand, and put it on the coffee table. He put his hand under my chin and turned it up. He slowly kissed me right on the lips. I felt like I should pull away, but then I remembered that I'd done the same thing for Henry earlier in the day.

Pulling me to his chest, I felt Mike's big hand on the back of my neck. It felt good there. We'd sat like this before, night after night, back when I was 20 and going through a real rough patch. I could remember it all, just like I felt like Mack had followed us home and was now sitting in the armchair that faced the front door. So many memories. I began to cry and couldn't stop.

. . .

At some point, I fell asleep and had a dream.

I was on the train. It was *The City of San Francisco*, the train that Carter and I had taken to Chicago back in '47. I was in the private car we'd rented and it was empty. I looked in all the compartments for Carter, but he was wasn't there. I walked through the connecting door into the next car and it was empty, too. I ran through the train and it was empty until I got to the car just behind the locomotive.

This was a Pullman car and each of the bedrooms was full and the doors were all closed. I could hear voices but I couldn't understand what any of them said. Surely Carter was in one of these rooms. I knocked on the door of the first room and a woman's voice said, "Come in."

I opened the door and there was my mother. Only, instead of the room being a small, modern Pullman bedroom, it was an ornate bedroom. She was sitting up in bed, just like I remembered from the summer of '29. Her light brown eyes were shining and her long brown hair was gathered loose over her left shoulder. Her beauty was breathtaking.

She smiled at me and I asked, "What are you doing here?" She didn't answer. I said, "I'm looking for Carter. Have you seen him?" She smiled. I knew she was happy, which was a relief, somehow. She pointed to her left and I knew she meant to try the next room, so I did.

When I opened that door, I was surprised and happy. The lower bed had been made and, sitting on it, in his tan uniform was Captain Ignacio Esparza, who liked to be called Nacho. I walked over and sat down next to him. I put my hand on his face and looked at his big mustache for a long moment and thought about kissing it. Looking up, I could see the light in his brown eyes and felt so happy to see him and be next to him. I took in a deep breath and remembered his aroma, which was sweet and spicy. He pulled me in a big squeeze and whispered, "Not here. Next door, I think." I nodded and found myself in another room.

This was the cramped room I'd shared with Mack on the ship back to San Francisco at the end of the war. I crawled up to the top bunk and there was Mack, looking just like he had in '45. He was in his BVDs, reading a magazine, and lying on top of a scratchy wool blanket. Somehow, I squeezed in next to him and asked, "Have you seen Carter?" He reached his arm around me and pulled me in tightly. I heard someone calling my name and, before I knew it, I was awake on the couch next to Mike.

Chapter 4

137 Hartford Street
Wednesday, June 16, 1954
Sometime that evening

Mike had kicked off his shoes while I'd been asleep and had propped his socked feet up on the coffee table. He had a book in his left hand and his right arm around me. It was one of the pulp novels that he liked so much. I stayed right where I was, with my head on his chest, and felt the rise and fall of his breath.

"How long was I asleep?" I asked.

He pulled me in closer and said, "About an hour, or so."

I pulled back and said, "Have you been sitting there all this time?"

He laughed. "No." He looked at me sideways. "That must have been some dream."

I nodded. It was vivid. I could see it like I could see any other memory.

"Wanna tell me about it?"

"I was looking for Carter."

"Did you find him?"

"No. I was on a train."

Mike laughed.

"What?"

"Was it going faster and faster?"

I laughed. "No. It was one of those dreams where you're looking for something and never find it."

I sat there for a moment. "My mother, Nacho, and Mack."

"How'd they look?" Releasing his grip on my shoulder, Mike leaned over and put the book on the table. He put his feet on the floor, stood up, and stretched.

"Alive."

He turned and looked down at me. "How'd that make you feel?"

"Happy."

He nodded and padded into the kitchen. I heard him open the icebox door. Then I heard him get a couple of glasses from the cabinet. "That Mrs. Kopek is some housekeeper. I've never seen this place so clean. You could eat off the floor."

I replied, "She's the best."

"How's Ike doing?" That was her son. Back at Christmas, we'd helped Ike when he'd been charged with a murder he didn't commit. His father had died in the process and his mother now worked as our housekeeper. She came in every day for a few hours and made everything shine.

"He's good. Carter and I are still dropping by over at Joe's Number 2 when we can." After the dust had cleared, we'd helped get Ike set up in his own business. He was the owner and manager of a gymnasium in

North Beach and was doing well. So far.

"There's some sort of meat pie in the oven. You want me to heat it up?"

My stomach growled in reply. "Yeah." I stood up, took off my coat and tie, and walked into the kitchen. As I did so, I noticed I had stopped shivering.

Mike said, "That's a good idea, Nick. I didn't know you two were being that conscientious. He's smart, that kid. I hope he stays on..." Mike paused. He grinned at me and said, "The right side of the law."

"You were gonna say, 'the straight and narrow,' right?"

He laughed. "As if that was even possible."

. . .

We sat at the kitchen table and consumed the entire pie by ourselves. Mrs. Kopek had also left a couple of bottles of Bohemian pilsner in the icebox. It was a home brew that a Czech friend of hers made and it was just about the best thing I'd ever tasted. We decided to split one bottle between us.

Mike took the last gulp from his glass, burped, and pushed his plate back. "That woman sure knows how to cook. She's almost as good as you." He smiled at me as he said that.

"Better. I don't know what some of the flavors are and she's slowly getting Carter used to garlic. It's a small miracle."

Mike pulled out a package of Lucky Strikes and offered me one. I shook my head. Using his own Zippo, he lit up and then looked at me.

"Why were you looking for Carter in the dream?"

I stood up and began to gather the plates and silverware. "I dunno. When he's not around, I miss him."

33

Right then, the phone rang. I looked up at the clock. It was 9:15.

Mike said, "Maybe that's him."

As I walked over to the phone, I said, "Maybe." I picked up the receiver and said, "Yeah?"

"Nick? It's Henry." His voice was shaking.

"What's wrong?"

"I just got a phone call."

"Who from?" I waved at Mike. He stood up and walked over to the alcove. I moved the phone out so he could hear.

"I don't know."

"What was it about?"

"It was some man. And it was about the dead guy."

"What'd he say?"

"He said that I should stay away from doing any investigating on my own. And that you should, too."

Mike took the phone out of my hand and said, "Henry. It's Mike."

I could hear Henry say, "What are you doing there?" It was oddly accusatory.

Mike just said, "Did you recognize the voice?"

"No. It sounded muffled."

"Can you repeat exactly what it said?"

"Um..." He was quiet for a moment. "It was something like, 'If you're smart, you won't investigate that little accident today. And you'll tell your buddy Williams the same thing. Got that?' And then whoever it was hung up."

"Is Robert there?" Mike asked.

"Yes."

"Put him on the phone."

"Sure." Henry sounded annoyed but he did what Mike asked.

"Hi, Mike. That was creepy."

"Look. I want you to help Henry pack a bag. He needs enough clothes for a few days and then you two head over to your place. Got that? And don't waste time. Get packed and get going. OK?"

"Sure, Mike. But--"

"No questions. Get packed and get out."

"Sure."

Mike put the receiver back in its cradle and looked down at me. "You and me, we're going upstairs and packing a bag for you and one for Carter. You're moving to the Mark Hopkins for a few days."

I didn't like the idea but I knew he was right.

. . .

Back in '47, a Chicago wise guy by the name of Nick DeJohn was rubbed out by a small group of local mobsters. One of them was the current boss, whose name was Michael Abati.

San Francisco wasn't Chicago or New York, that was for sure. The cops had, for many years, kept the local wise guys in their place and made sure no one from out of town moved in. Just like down in L.A. But that didn't mean Abati didn't have muscle. Mike's response to all of this meant he suspected Abati had just squeezed one of his own, Johnny Russell, the guy who was pushed off the top of my office building.

He could have been wrong but Mike was a level-headed Joe. Always had been. So, if he said move, I moved. And that's what I did.

By midnight, I was in a two-bedroom suite at the Mark Hopkins. My revolver was loaded and by the bed as I stretched out to make some calls.

The first one was to Marnie. After eight rings, she picked up.

"Sorry to call you so late, doll."

"No problem, Nick." I could hear her yawn. Then I heard a male voice followed by the sound of her hand covering the phone's mouthpiece. I smiled. I was glad she was with this new guy, who's name I never could remember.

Finally, she asked, "What's up?"

"I had to go buy some bread." That was an old code we'd come up with a while ago. It meant I was hiding out. The night manager had agreed, after a good talking-to by Mike, to let me register under an assumed name. As far as the registration book said, I was, "Robert Parnell." I'd used that name before.

"Go buy some... Oh. Gotcha. Will I see you tomorrow?"

"Probably. Just wanted to let you know. Sleep tight." I couldn't resist. "Don't let the bed bug bite. Unless you want him to."

She hung up on me.

My next call was long distance to Santa Paula. The gal at the front desk of the little motel down there wasn't happy about getting a switchboard call but she put me through anyway.

"Hiya, Chief."

"Hi, Nick. What's up?" Carter's voice was muffled.

"I wanted to call and tell you that I had to go to the store and get some bread."

"What?" I'd told him the code a while ago and I hoped he remembered.

"The store. I had to leave and go to the store. You know. For bread."

There was a long pause. "Oh, right." Another pause. "Are you OK?" Now he was awake.

"Yeah. I'm fine. I'll meet you at the office tomorrow. When do you think you'll be back?"

"Might be 7."

"If I'm not in the office, I'll be down at the Hangover."

"Got it. Should I be worried?"

"Nope. Just drive safe and get home because you know how I'm feeling right now."

There was a long silence. "I know. Me, too."

"Night, Chief."

"G'night, Boss."

With that, the line went dead. I waited to hear what happened. About two seconds later, I heard a second click. I was assuming it was the desk clerk at the motel. Or, at least that's what I was hoping.

. . .

As I lay there in the darkness of the room, the lights of the City illuminated the ceiling. I couldn't sleep, so I stood up, walked over to the tall window, and looked out over this place that I loved and where I felt at home.

It had its problems. No place was perfect. But there was no place quite like the City. I was part of it and, even though I didn't understand it, I felt like I had to live in San Francisco. My fate was tied up with its own. This was all ridiculous, of course. I smiled at my high-flying thoughts. I wondered what Carter would make of all my musings. He probably would have laughed and kissed me to get me to stop, more than anything.

Then I thought about Michael Abati and realized I was probably in his sights now. I wondered what that would mean to the cops. This would be a perfect deal for them. Let Abati take care of me and my little gang of queers. The City would be saved from our perversion and everyone would be happy. It was a morbid thought and, even though I'd seen plenty of death in my life, I didn't dwell on the what-might-happen unless I needed to. And worrying about the penny-ante mobsters of San Francisco wasn't high on my list of concerns, truth be told.

The construction on the building would continue. I was worth more to the mob alive than dead. This wasn't gonna be my last construction project. There would be more payoffs to come. They didn't ask for much and I had more than enough.

I walked back over to the bed, picked up my pack of Camels on the night table, and shook out the next available cigarette. I flicked my Zippo open like I'd learned to do in the Navy and quickly lit up. As I flipped the lid closed, I thought I heard a sound in the hallway.

I quickly stubbed out my cigarette and grabbed my gun. Even though I was just in my BVDs, I moved from the bedroom to the living room of the suite. I slowly crept down the marble entrance hallway in my bare feet. Holding my gun in the air, I stopped and listened at the door.

"Are you sure?" asked one voice.

"Parnell," said another voice. "That's his old man's first name." Well, that alias would have to be put to rest.

These were two male voices and they were whispering. They were so close to the door that I could smell the breath from one of them. He needed to brush more often.

I heard the scrape of something metallic being inserted into the lock in order to force it open. I backed up into the corner as I heard the lock click. I could see the door knob because the dim light from outside the living room windows was reflected off it. I watched the door knob slowly turn and shifted the gun in my hand so I was holding it by the barrel instead of the handle.

A sliver of light from the hallway began to widen as

the door quietly opened. A thick, squat form slowly walked across the marble floor. His leather-soled shoes squeaked softly as he did.

His buddy walked in right behind him. As fast as I could, I pistol-whipped the buddy on his neck. As he fell with a thud, I managed to do the same to the first guy before he had time to respond.

I went to the tall drapes that were covering the high windows of the living room. I yanked hard on the cords that opened and closed them. The whole setup came crashing down. It took a minute, but I managed to pull the cords out of the mechanism and then used them to bind the arms and legs of the two guys who were prone on the floor. Once that was done, I went into the bedroom and grabbed a handkerchief from my trousers. Returning to the entrance hallway, I checked for pulses, just in case. They each had one.

The squat guy had dropped his piece. Using the handkerchief, I picked it up and emptied the bullets. I put all of that on a table by the window.

I went back to his partner. He had fallen on his face, which only a mother could love, and there was a gash on his forehead from where he hit the marble. He was bleeding and it was running down the side of his head.

I ran into the bathroom and grabbed a small towel from the stack on the counter. I ran it under the water for a moment and then walked back to the ugly mug and pressed the towel on the wound to hopefully staunch the bleeding. I held it there for a couple of minutes until the bleeding stopped.

I reached over and, using my handkerchief, grabbed the barrel of his gun, stood up, and walked over to the table to add it to the other one.

Then, and only then, did I pull on my clothes and call the hotel security office. In that order.

"How did you know they were there?" That was Lieutenant Holland. We were standing in the living room of my hotel suite. The hotel security had called him at my insistence. Mike was sitting on one of the sofas, keeping quiet and taking it all in. He was the second call I had made.

"I had just lit a cigarette in the bedroom and I heard a sound."

"And your gun?"

"Licensed. I was carrying it with me in case something like this happened."

"What about your P.I. license? I thought it was suspended."

"The board cleared me in January and it's been reinstated."

The lieutenant was wearing the same London Fog coat he'd had on earlier in the day. But now his coat and trousers were blue and he had on a yellow tie.

"You're lucky you didn't kill either of them. How'd you know to hit them on the neck and not the skull."

Mike said, "I taught him that."

The lieutenant frowned and looked down at Mike. "When?"

I answered, "When I was living with him and he was teaching me how to take care of myself."

A look of distaste mixed with something I couldn't read passed over the man's face. He looked at his notebook and made a couple of notes.

"Why are you staying here?"

"It was Mike's suggestion and I agreed with him. Henry Winters called me after he received a threatening phone call. He went to stay with a friend and I came over here."

40

The lieutenant looked over at Mike. "When were you going to tell me about those calls?" There was a tone of annoyance in his voice along with, again, something I couldn't read.

Mike said, "First thing in the morning. Didn't seem like enough to call down to the station and make a report. They were hunches with no evidence."

"But you thought your hunch was significant enough to warrant moving your friends?"

"I know Abati. If it was him, I know that he doesn't fool around."

The lieutenant scribbled something in his notebook but didn't respond.

He looked up at me. "How do you think they knew to find you?"

"That's a good question. They could have followed us when we drove over here from Eureka Valley. Someone at the switchboard here could have been listening when I made a couple of calls."

"Who did you call?"

"My secretary, Marnie Wilson." He started scribbling again.

"What did you tell her?"

"That I'd gone out for bread."

The lieutenant looked up. "What?"

"That's a code we use that means I'm hiding out."

"Huh. Who else did you call?"

"Carter Jones. He's down in Santa Paula with a couple of employees. They're helping the local fire department with an arson investigation."

"What did you tell Mr. Jones?"

"Same thing. Someone was listening in on that call. I heard a click after he hung up. He's at a little motel so it might have been the person at the switchboard down there. Or, it could have been here."

"And, didn't you check in under an alias?"

"Yes. Robert Parnell. But they knew that was me, somehow."

"Parnell?"

"My father's first name. And they knew that."

The lieutenant scribbled a while longer. Finally, he asked, "Where do you go now?"

I took a deep breath. "Since it's almost dawn, I'm going to the office."

Mike said, "First, we go check on Henry."

I nodded. "Yeah."

"Where will you stay tonight?" That was the lieutenant.

I had a sudden idea which surprised me but immediately made sense. It was probably the best solution. "I have a place we can hole up where no one will find us."

"Where is that?"

I smiled and said, "If I told you then you'd be able to find us, wouldn't you?"

The lieutenant nodded. "Fair enough. I'd rather know but I can always reach you through your office, right?"

I nodded. "Day and night. We have a service and I'll stay in touch with them after business hours."

The lieutenant closed his notebook. "Let me warn you, Mr. Williams. I don't like rogue private dicks who shadow the cops. You have a reputation for doing that." I stood there and listened. He looked down at Mike. "And I don't work at the North Station, so I ain't one of your buddies. You call me when you have something you need to report but I don't meet for chats over coffee. Got that?"

Mike stood up and said, "Fair enough."

The lieutenant nodded and was gone.

42

. . .

On the way out, we stopped at the front desk. The first shift was just coming in and they all looked a little dazed. I asked the first one I saw, "Who's the manager on duty right now?"

She replied, "Mr. Olander." That was who we'd talked to earlier when I'd checked in. "But he's busy right now."

"With the police?"

Her eyes widened but she replied, "I'm afraid I don't know."

I smiled and said, "I'm Mr. Williams. I'm checking out of my suite. Are you sure he can't see me?"

She looked doubtful but said, "Just one moment and I'll call." She walked over to a phone on the wall, picked it up, and said, "Hotel Manager, please."

I looked around the grand lobby. It was quiet, which wasn't surprising since it was just past 6 in the morning.

I heard the clerk say, "There's a Mr. Williams checking out and he wants to speak with you." She turned her back to us as she listened. She said, "Yes, sir," and then put the receiver on the hook.

She walked back to the counter, smiled, and said, "I really am sorry. Mr. Olander is busy. Is there somewhere he can reach you?"

Ignoring the question, I put the key on the counter. "You'll need to send someone in to check the damage to the living room drapes. Just send the bill to my office. Mr. Olander will know all about it." I wanted to declare, like the great Caruso, that I would never return. But I knew I would. It was the Mark Hopkins, after all. Before she could reply, Mike and I walked through the lobby and out into the early morning light.

43

Chapter 5

Offices of Consolidated Security
Thursday, June 17, 1954
Around 10 in the morning

Henry wasn't happy and I couldn't blame him.

"And to top it all off, Universal has put a stop-work order out for the site."

I was at my desk. Henry was in one chair. Mike was in the other. Robert was leaning in the doorway. And, Marnie, as always, was listening from her desk.

"Is that what the call from Pam was about?" I asked.

"Yes."

"Who pays for that?" I asked.

Henry was indignant. "I'm not. And neither are you. Universal wants to renege on their contract, then they pay."

I said, "But it shouldn't land on the heads of the guys at the site. They should get paid."

He shook his head and said, "I wish I was back at

45

Bechtel just working on drawings and estimates."

I looked at him straight-on. "Really?"

He looked away. "No, of course not." There was a trace of bitterness in his voice. "They wouldn't have me back, anyway." He'd been fired the previous summer because a background check revealed his proclivities. The project he was scheduled to work on for several years required a security clearance he wouldn't be able to get. And, besides, they didn't like having a queer in their midst. Or, that's what I'd heard.

Robert asked, "Is Pam in any danger?"

I shook my head. "I don't think so. When I talked to her early this morning, she and Diane hadn't received any calls. I told her to keep an eye and an ear open and to let us know if anything happened. But, so far, so good." Pam lived with Diane, a schoolteacher. They were our next-door neighbors. Carter referred to them as a "lady couple." They also had two annoying dogs that I ignored but who adored Carter. Like everyone else.

Mike snorted. "That's an advantage to her being a girl in construction. No one is taking her seriously."

Henry shook his head. "The men on that site do. She knows her stuff. That gal is the only reason we are ahead of schedule."

I looked around the room. "I have a plan for where Henry, Carter, and I are going to hole up for the next few days. We're gonna let the cops do their job and we'll keep our heads down. I still have to make one phone call. Mike and I are gonna walk over to the phone booth at the corner of Hyde and then we'll be back. Let's meet back here in fifteen."

We all stood up. "Oh, and Henry?"

"Yes, Nick?"

"Call Universal and set up a meeting at noon. I wanna

find out what the hell Rutledge is up to."

He shrugged and said, "Sure."

. . .

"I'm still not sure what to call you." I was in the phone booth at Hyde and Bush. Mike was standing nearby, looking nonchalant as he read the Chronicle. I was talking to my father's new wife, and Marnie's mother, the former Mrs. Wilson.

"You could call me 'mother,' if you'd like, Nicholas."

Before I could help myself, I sighed.

She quickly said, "How about Lettie? That was my nickname in school. And I always liked it."

"Are you sure?" I asked. She was a stickler for protocol.

"Yes. Lettie it is." There was a brief pause on the line. "Is that the only reason you called?"

"No, it's not. Did you see this morning's papers?"

"If you're referring to that awful business at your building site, then yes. Are you involved in that?"

"In a way. It's a long story but Henry got a threatening call last night. Mike had us move but a couple of toughs tracked me down early this morning."

"Are you hurt?"

"No. But they're not doing very well."

Lettie snickered on the other end of the line. It gave me a secret thrill. "I never wish harm on anyone, but I can tell you I would enjoy seeing you 'lay out some toughs' someday."

I laughed heartily at that. "Well, I hope you never get the chance. But I appreciate your confidence."

"I suppose, then, that you want to move your little gang over here?"

"That's it in a nutshell."

"How many?"

"Well, there'd be Henry and Robert. Carter and myself. And then we'd need Mike to stay with us for added protection."

Proving once again what an amazing woman she was, Lettie said, "You can all move into the top floor. There are three rooms up there. I'll get those set up today. When should we expect you?"

"I'll send Henry and Robert over to help you."

"Nonsense. I can manage with the staff."

"Henry doesn't have anything to do. And Robert... Well, he's amazing. There's not anything he can't do."

"So, what you're saying is that they need to do a little work to earn their keep?"

I laughed again. "Sure. That's a good way to put it." I took in a deep breath. "What do you think my father will say?"

"You leave Parnell to me, Nicholas."

I said, "Thanks, Lettie."

"My pleasure. However, I must tell you that dinner will be served promptly at 6. If any of your group arrives late, it will be sandwiches in the kitchen. I can be flexible, but only to a point, dear."

. . .

There was a mild uproar at the office when I explained the plan. But, after everyone talked it out, it became the obvious solution and for one reason: my feud with my father was legendary. Although the wedding had, in many ways, been the biggest social event of the year to date, the casual observer would have thought we were still not on speaking terms. No one would think of looking for me there.

"Robert. You go first. Take Sam with you to your apartment, just in case." Sam was a big weight lifter we'd hired last Christmas. He was also Ike's squeeze.

"Take a cab over here and drop him off. Then have the driver drop you off at the back of the Pacific Union Club. It's half a block from there. Got that?"

He nodded. "What should I do when I get there?"

"Take charge of getting the third floor set up. I've told my..." I paused. "Marnie's mother to expect you. And I told her about your whiz-bang skills. Those rooms have been closed off since '29, so there's probably a lot of work to be done."

I looked at Henry. "Mike is going with us to meet Rutledge at Universal. Then we'll take you to Sacramento Street and get you smuggled in, somehow. He and I will come back here and wait for Carter, Martinelli, and Ray to get back from Santa Paula."

"Then what?" asked Marnie.

"Then we let the cops do their job."

Marnie looked at me as if she didn't quite believe me. I winked and said, "Dinner is at 6 tonight. Don't be late."

She smiled. "I've known my mother all my life. I won't."

. . .

"I'm sure you're here about the stop-work order I issued for 600 Market Street."

Henry, Mike, and I were seated on one side of a large table in a conference room with a view of the bay. Rutledge and a man he'd introduced as William Troyer sat on the other. Troyer was taking over for Vernon Keller who was no longer working at Universal.

"Yes," I said. "What's going on?"

"Well, with the departure of Mr. Keller, I needed some time to bring Mr. Troyer up to speed with where the project is."

I asked, "The fastest way to do that is for him to meet

with Pam Spaulding."

Troyer shifted uncomfortably in his chair. He was a little older than me. His chestnut hair was slicked back from his wide face. His belly was pressing on his shirt, straining the buttons. He looked uncomfortable in a coat and tie. He reminded me of the Seabees. Those were the Navy construction guys I'd known in New Guinea during the war. He probably had been one.

"About that," said Rutledge. "I don't think you need to have the additional budget expense of having two construction managers. Troyer here can manage the job site on his own."

I shook my head. "Nope. The contract says in black and white that the site will be managed by the person designated by Winters Engineering."

Rutledge looked at Henry, who nodded. "I know you're new to the game, Winters, but isn't it unusual for the building owner to make these kind of decisions?"

Henry, who seemed to have come alive now that Keller was out of the picture, said, "Well, it's like this, Mr. Rutledge. Nick is a major shareholder in Winters Engineering. When I was dumped by Bechtel, he put up the money for me to start my own firm."

Rutledge looked at me. A wave of distaste passed over his face. He muttered, "Birds of a feather..."

Mike cracked his knuckles meaningfully and put on his monster face. "That's right, Mr. Rutledge. We tend to flock together."

Rutledge sat up in his chair. Troyer looked like he was raring for a fight, but Rutledge just said, "Well, if it's in the contract, then that's that. I'm sure Mrs. Spaulding--"

"Miss Spaulding," I corrected him.

"Oh, I see. Well, I'm sure that will be just fine. Don't

you think, Troyer?"

The man looked at me with an intense hatred and said, "Sure thing, Mr. Rutledge."

"So, back to the matter at hand," I said.

"Yes. About that stop-work order." Rutledge cleared his throat and said, "How about we resume on Monday? That should give us plenty of time."

"And what about the pay?" I asked.

"What pay?" That was Troyer.

"Will the men on the job site be paid for today and tomorrow?"

Rutledge said, "That's covered in the union contract. If there's a stop-work and they're idled, then, for those two days, their pay goes to a floor minimum."

I nodded. "I'll cover the difference."

Troyer looked over at me in surprise. His face relaxed a little.

Rutledge shook his head. "Oh, no, Mr. Williams. This is a standard union contract. It's customary."

I said, "No man working on any job for me is gonna have to lose a penny because you're a coward."

I watched as Rutledge's face turned red. "Coward?"

"Sure. You don't think we all know that someone is squeezing you? I don't know why and I don't care why, but if you think that stopping work for these couple of days will buy you time, that's fine. But those men working on the job get paid their usual wages. And I'll make up the difference between that and the minimum."

I noticed that Troyer was nodding his head thoughtfully as I said all that.

. . .

My father's house sat at the corner of Sacramento and Taylor. After the meeting, we drove up California

Street. Instead of turning right at Mason, as I normally would have, I stayed on California until we got to Leavenworth. Turning right, I proceeded up to Clay and turned right again. By this time, Mike and I were convinced we weren't being tailed. Keeping both eyes open, I drove the couple of blocks to Taylor, made another right, and then dropped Henry off at the corner of Sacramento. We saw him enter the house without incident and headed back to the office.

. . .

"How goes it over there?" I had Lettie on the phone. It was just past 5 in the afternoon. Carter had called in from San Jose. He thought they would be at the office at 6:30.

"Just fine. You were right. That Robert is amazing. I think you'll be quite pleased with what we found once we opened up all the rooms."

"The only thing I remember up there is that each room had the same bedspread made of satin and each was a different color."

"Yes! Your mother had wonderful taste! There's a pink room, a green room, and a blue room."

As if I could hear my mother talking, I said, "Rose, Emerald, and Sapphire."

Lettie drew in a breath. "Of course! How clever! And, it's all quite splendid. Everything was tucked away in hermetically sealed bags. We didn't even need to wash the sheets. They smelled just like lavender."

"How did my father take the news?"

"Oh, you know how he is. He's puffing away on his pipe in his office and I'm pretending like he's not upset. But," she paused for a moment. "I'm sure he'll be quite happy to have both you and Carter staying here these next few days. You know, Nicholas." She took in a

52

breath and quietly said, "If I didn't know your father better, I would say that he has a *pash*, as we used to call it, for Carter."

I laughed and said, "You missed the funeral last year when Carter carried him full body through the cathedral. I don't think the old man has been the same since."

With a mixture of humor and reproach, Lettie said, "Please be more respectful of your father in the future."

I couldn't help myself. "Yes, ma'am."

. . .

Mike and I were by ourselves. I'd sent Marnie over to the house so she could get there on time to have dinner with everyone. The rest of the guys had gone home for the day.

Mike had his big shoes up on my desk and his hands behind his head. "So, I've been thinking about our conversation last night."

"Yeah?" I had been reading some mail that I needed to catch up on.

"How you feeling today about Carter?"

"I miss him like hell."

"You know, Nick." Mike looked up at the ceiling. "Things happen in our lives. Sometimes we're rolling along, happy as a clam. But, most of the time, we're just dodging and weaving and trying not to get sucker-punched by whatever is happening."

I looked up and smirked. "What are you saying, O Wise One?"

He put his feet on the floor and smiled. "What I'm saying, you little pissant, is that not every moment is golden. You're a graduate of the Hard Knocks School. You know what I mean."

I nodded. "I guess I thought when I finally knew what happened to my mother, that life would be different."

Mike leaned in. "Life is different. You have the most goddam wonderful husband."

I smiled when he used that word. I thought Carter and I were the only ones to use it.

"Yeah. I said it. Husband." He stood up and tucked in the back of his shirt into his trousers. "You and Carter are fucking married and, let me tell you, there ain't a man in this goddam building who isn't stone-cold jealous."

I nodded. "So, what you're saying is that I need to stop whining like a little baby and man up. I'm rich, I have the most handsome husband in North America. Hell, I even own a boat and two goddam planes. What's to complain about?" I got a little heated at the end.

"No, Nick. What I'm saying is that when you notice a rose, stop and fucking smell it. When your husband comes through that door, you knock everyone out of your way and jump into his arms and shower him with kisses. He deserves it for putting up with you for seven lousy years."

His voice had softened at the end. I got to my feet, moved a chair close to him, and stood up on it. I pulled him close, put my arms around his neck, looked down into his striking blue eyes, and said, "You're right, Mike. And, let me remind you that you're the best friend a guy ever had." I kissed him on the lips and then held his head against mine for a long while.

. . .

About 7, I heard the trudge of weary feet walking down the hall from the elevator. Mike was reading one of his pulp novels while I was just about done going through my mail.

I looked up as the door opened. Carter Jones, himself, walked through the door. He walked in and said, "Hello, honey. I'm home."

I got up and walked right into his arms. "I missed you so goddam much, Carter. I'm glad you're back."

He reached down and kissed me. As he did, my eyes got wet.

"Hey."

I just shook my head. "It's nothing. Just happy to see you, Chief."

We kissed for a long moment until Mike cleared his throat. "Where's Ray?"

Carter looked confused. "I dropped him off at your place. I thought you knew that."

I glanced up at Mike who looked upset for a moment. "Oh, sure." He closed his eyes for a beat and then opened them. I couldn't tell for sure, but they looked wet to me. He sighed and then asked, "Can I get some of that?"

I smiled and made room for Mike and Carter to exchange hugs. Mike kissed Carter on the cheek, something I'd never seen him do before. Carter looked down at me over Mike's shoulder and said, "What's been going on here? Everyone is so affectionate. We were only gone two nights."

Mike said, "Come on in and we'll tell you all about it."

. . .

Before we'd left the office, my father had called.

"Don't forget, Nicholas, that there's a garage under this house."

"I had forgotten." It hadn't been there when I'd left home in '39. It wasn't that I'd forgotten. I didn't know about it.

55

"It's on Sacramento. There's a buzzer. Leticia just had one of those two-way intercoms installed. You press the button and, well, I'm sure you know how that sort of thing works."

"Yes, Father. Thanks for the reminder. Sorry we missed dinner."

"Well, things being what they are, I'm sure we can overlook that." I wasn't sure but I thought I heard some humor in his voice.

"See you in a few minutes, Father."

"That'll be fine, Nicholas."

. . .

I pulled the Buick into a space next to a Cadillac. It was a '54 and looked new. We brought our things up the stairs and into the kitchen. It was spotless, of course, but empty. I could hear Perry Como coming from somewhere in the house. We walked into the dining room from the kitchen and then into the large sitting room. Robert and Henry were dancing with Marnie and Lettie while my father was sitting in his favorite leather chair watching the whole thing and smoking his pipe.

I said, "Howdy, folks."

Lettie smiled at Henry as he released her. She walked over and gave me a kiss on the cheek. Carter leaned down for the same. I said, "You remember Mike from the wedding."

She smiled, offered her hand, and said, "Of course."

I hadn't really thought this thing through completely. I'd forgotten that Mike had only ever met my father twice. The first time was back in '40 when they'd had a huge fight about my living with Mike. The second time was last May when Mike had still been a police lieutenant and had witnessed my father shoot a man in self-defense. Mike had been at the wedding but didn't speak to my father. And that had been on purpose.

My father stood up, walked over, and shook Carter's hand. He patted me on the arm and then said, "Lieutenant Robertson, I've never had the chance to thank you for being so kind to me last year."

Everyone in the room stopped what they were doing, except Perry Como, of course, who kept singing on the record player. Mike turned red from embarrassment and said, "It's good to see you again, Dr. Williams."

They both shook and my father said, "You never saw what all the fuss was about last year, did you?"

"No, sir."

"Well, come into my office and let me show you."

I was shocked. As they walked towards my father's office, I followed them as did Carter. I heard Lettie say to the rest, "One more time around the room, shall we?"

When we walked into the office, the first thing I noticed was that the Persian rug, which had been much older than me, was gone. The inlaid wood floor underneath had been restored and was polished to a shine. In the center of the room was an octagonal table that looked to be made of teak. It could have been Chinese. Or, more likely, it had been made to look Chinese. It covered the exact location of the safe in the floor and hid it perfectly.

The legs must have been on wheels because, when my father pushed on the table, it effortlessly moved across the floor revealing the safe door. I noticed it has been replaced since I'd last seen it sometime in the 30s.

"My knees aren't what they were. Can you help me get down there, Carter?"

I watched as Carter bent down on one knee and held

my father's arm as he knelt on the floor in front of the safe. Leaning down, he twirled the dials several time and then turned them to five numbers before I heard a click. There must have been some hidden mechanism, because the door almost effortlessly lifted off the floor.

Mike was standing next to Carter. They both gasped. I walked over and looked inside. It was shocking to behold. There were trays of gold bars, stacks and stacks of bundled cash, and an assortment of rubies, emeralds, sapphires, and diamonds.

Carter looked up at me and shook his head in amazement. I said, "I don't remember it being this full."

My father leaned on Carter and then pulled himself up off the floor. "I've had a bit of luck in the last year or so. I didn't know investing in lumber would be as lucrative as it's turned out to be." He stood up straight and proper, as always. "I'm finally back up to the level I prefer."

I knew that was at least two million because last year he'd complained about being down to a mere million. From what I could see, it might be more than that.

. . .

"I'm hungry." That was Carter.

We were watching Lettie and Henry dance the Lindy Hop to a 78 of "In The Mood." They both were really good. Lettie could swing better than any bobby soxer.

Mike was standing next to Carter and said, "Me, too."

"Follow me, gents." I led them into the kitchen as the song came to an end and everyone clapped.

I was going through the icebox when I heard Mrs. Young ask, "Sandwiches?"

I felt like I'd been caught stealing. My face went red and I looked up. Everyone else laughed.

"Sit you down." We all did just that. "Seems to me you were always partial to Burgie, Mr. Nick."

I nodded. "Is there some in the cooler?" There was a large cooler behind the kitchen where vegetables, hams, beer, and the like were kept.

"Yes. Go help yourself."

I stood up, walked down the hall, and pulled open the big walk-in cooler. As if it was 1938, I reflexively grabbed the long stick that we put in the door latch so it wouldn't close. I quickly grabbed three bottles of Burgie and left as fast as I could. I never liked going in there.

When I walked back into the kitchen, the table was set with three small plates, three napkins, and three glasses. I walked over to the end of one of the counters and popped the tops off the bottles.

As I sat down, Mrs. Young said, "It's ham, Swiss cheese, tomatoes, pickle relish, and mustard on cottage loaf."

I said, "That sounds great, Mrs. Young. Thank you. You don't have to--"

"My room is right downstairs, as I'm sure you remember, and I'd be worrying about my kitchen if I was to leave you to your own devices."

Mike looked at me as he poured out his beer and guffawed.

"Oh, I remember you, Patrolman Robertson."

Mike and I both blushed. Carter looked at us and asked, "What's this?"

Mrs. Young said, "I swore to never speak of it."

Carter looked at me. "Well?"

I shrugged. "It was a long time ago."

Mike put down his glass and leaned back in his chair. "It was all my fault. I'll tell the story."

I blushed again. "The clean version, if you please."

Carter's eyebrows went up.

I nodded, looked at Mrs. Young, whose back was turned, and put my finger to my lips.

He smiled and mouthed, "Later."

Mike said, "It was in the summer of 1939."

Mrs. Young said, "And he was up to his tricks. Petty thieving and such."

I shook my head. "Not me, your honor. I was innocent."

Mike crossed his arms and looked at me. "Framed by the gang. That's still your story?"

"It wasn't a gang. It was those kids that had been kicked out of St. Ignatius with me."

Carter smiled. "You never did finish, did you?"

I shook my head. "Nope."

"Anyway," said Mike, "I was in trouble myself. I'd been pulled off motorcycle patrol in June and was assigned to foot patrol for three months."

"What was that about?" asked Carter.

Not wanting to offend Mrs. Young, I quickly said, "Let's skip that part."

Mike smiled and said, "So, there I was, minding my own business walking down Mission Street, when I walk into a den of hoodlums up to no good."

Carter smirked, "South of the Slot, Nick?"

I replied, "Does anything good ever happen down there?" That was an old joke.

"What were they up to?" asked Carter, who was having a lot more fun with this than he should.

"Petty thievery!" declared Mrs. Young as she put a plate of sandwiches in front of us. She walked over, opened the icebox, and pulled out a can of Lucky beer.

I took a sandwich and put it on my plate. "Jerry Howzer was the thief. He'd lifted some candy bars from a corner store."

"That's it?" asked Carter.

I shook my head. "No. There were other things. But, it was all petty. We were all 17 and thought we were hot stuff. We all had allowances and none of us were gonna go hungry. We were just bored."

Mrs. Young sat down with her can of beer and opened it with a church key she pulled out of her apron. "That was always the trouble. I told Zelda once, if I told her a thousand times, that your problem was that the school had nothing to teach you. You were always too smart."

I shrugged. "I wanted out." I said that quietly.

Mike sighed and took a bite of his sandwich.

"Well, that's as may be. All I know is that a policeman's boots make a loud racket on a wood floor."

Carter looked up at Mike. "What?"

"What happened was that I caught this gang of scofflaws and hauled them into the Mission Station."

Mrs. Young added, "Where a kindly sergeant gave you boys a second chance."

"What was his name?" I asked Mike.

"Gustafson."

"Oh, right. Big Swede. Thick mustache." I blushed again, which Carter caught. His eyes looked at me for a long moment. I asked, "Whatever happened to him?"

Mike said, "Retired back in '49. Last I heard, he lives on Lake Arrowhead down in the southland."

I took a drink of my beer. "So, he releases us to our parents."

Mrs. Young hooked her thumb towards the dining room. "Certain parties overreacted a bit, if you don't mind me saying, Mr. Nick."

I smiled and said, "That's an understatement."

Mike looked at Carter. "The sergeant pulled me aside and asked me to keep an eye on this group."

"And, you did," I added, trying to keep the innuendo out of my voice.

Mike bit into his sandwich and smiled wolfishly. I blushed again.

With a peaches and cream accent, Carter said, "This is the most fascinatin' conversation I do think I've ever had."

"Anyway," I said, "I figured out Mike's usual patrol route and began to show up when I knew he would be there." I took another sip of beer. "Truth was, he was the first man who'd ever shown any interest in who I was."

Mrs. Young sighed. She stood up and took another can of Lucky from the icebox. As she opened that can, she said, "There was an awful lot that happened here that wasn't right. If it hadn't been for Zelda..." She didn't finish her sentence and took a drink from her can.

I nodded and said, "Yeah."

Mike said, "So, I began to notice that this spoiled brat of a kid might have more to hisself than met the eye. I started meeting him after my shift at a diner near the Mission Station. I'd buy him a grilled cheese and let him pour out his heart." He smiled at me and added, "Poor kid."

I looked down at the table. I could feel that familiar affection I had for Mike. I didn't want to embarrass Mrs. Young, but I had a strong urge to go sit in Mike's lap like I'd done long ago.

Carter asked, "The only part of this story that I've ever heard was that Mike got caught one night bringing Nick home."

I nodded. "One of those kids thought it would be fun to throw a party at this abandoned warehouse South of the Slot. It was a Saturday night and..." I looked at Mrs.

Young, whose mouth was already turned in disapproval, and decided to keep my mouth shut on the specifics. "It was a big shindig and we did a lot of stupid things. Someone called the cops. Several, including Mike, showed up and broke up the party. I don't know how we didn't go to jail, but we didn't. I could barely stand and Mike walked me home."

"From where?"

"Somewhere on Brannan. That's all I remember."

Mike said, "The kid's father owned the building. It's a factory now. Corner of 6th and Brannan."

"So, you walked Nick all the way up here from Brannan Street?"

Mike nodded.

"And that's when all hell broke loose!" Mrs. Young was obviously getting tipsy from the beer.

"I had to go through Nick's pockets to find his key."

Carter grinned. I shook my head.

Mike continued, "We walk in here and I guess I woke up Mrs. Young."

"You were banging around like a bunch of monkeys. I knew it wasn't burglars from the noise. But I found my baseball bat and was surprised as all get out to find a gigantic cop standing in my kitchen." She giggled and finished the last of her beer.

"What happened?" asked Carter.

"His nibs got thrown out, that's what." Mrs. Young looked like she was going to go for another beer.

Mike stood up and said, "Mrs. Young, can I help you downstairs? I've always wondered about the sound of the floor up here."

"Sure, you can. I know you well enough to know I'm perfectly safe."

She tottered across the kitchen to the back stairs with Mike holding her arm.

Once they were gone, Carter asked, "What happened?"

"Mike and I were making out in here is what happened. Mrs. Young came in about the same time as my father and that was the end of my misbegotten youth. He threw me out on my ass and Mike took me home. I don't know why Parnell didn't call the Mission Station and report Mike, but he didn't. Of course--"

Right then, Lettie poked her head around the kitchen door. "Oh, good. I wanted to make sure you had some dinner."

I stood up, feeling like I'd been caught again. "Mrs. Young made sandwiches for us."

She looked at me and then at Carter. "And I suppose Mr. Robertson is helping her to bed?"

I nodded.

She sighed. "She does like her Lucky."

. . .

The third floor was more narrow than the rest of the house. It was a row of four large rooms that ran the length of the Sacramento Street side of the house. The rooms were connected by a long hallway. Each room faced south. From the bedrooms, you could see the park across the street and the Huntington Hotel beyond that. The old Flood Mansion, now the Pacific Union Club, was just to the left.

Carter and I were in the Emerald Room. This was the one at the end of the hall. The large bathroom was between us and the Sapphire Room where Mike was camping out. The Rose Room at the top of the stairs was where Henry and Robert were sleeping.

We had both stripped down to our BVDs and I was feeling antsy. Carter was in bed, reading the privately published book he'd given my father at Christmas. It

64

was about the Gold Rush and included a chapter on my great-grandfather. The chrome lamp next to him was the only light in the room

I walked over and looked out the windows to see the view and to also check if there was anyone watching the house. I stood behind the long silk curtains and couldn't see anything suspicious outside.

The room was the height of Art Deco style. The satin bedspread had diamond patterns stitched into it. The furniture was all dark wood, square in shape, and had the usual Art Deco touches.

An eight-foot tall wardrobe with a mother-of-pearl diamond-shaped inlay across the doors was the centerpiece of the room. The wood was probably mahogany. And the contrast of the dark wood with the white and creamy color of the inlay was beautiful.

I turned around and crossed over to the bed. I sat down on my side and pulled my feet up.

"What's wrong?"

I looked over at Carter. He was propped up against the dark headboard. His bare chest was ruddy in the glow of the chrome lamp. The warmth of the light showed off the bits of red in his otherwise blonde chest hair.

I said, "This is the first time I've slept in this house since 19 fucking 39. That's fifteen goddam years. Almost half my life."

Carter closed the book and put it on the table. He reached over and pulled me close. He lifted up the covers to invite me to slide into the bed next to him, which I did. Once I was in the crook of his arm, he reached over and turned out the light. The dim lights of Huntington Park cast shadows in the room.

Running his hand up and down my arm, Carter said, "I think you're nervous because this is the first time you've slept with me while your father is under the same roof."

Of course, he was right.

Chapter 6

1198 Sacramento Street
Friday, June 18, 1954
Early morning

I awoke from a dream with a start. The house was quiet. I looked around the big bedroom and everything was where it was supposed to be. Carter was on his stomach and his right arm was flung across my chest.

I gently lifted it and slid off the bed.

"What?" was his sleepy question.

"I'm gonna call the service." I walked over to pull on my trousers and put on my shirt.

"Wait and I'll go with you."

I finished buttoning my trousers and started doing the same to my shirt. I didn't need shoes just to go downstairs. "No, you sleep. I'll be back in five."

"M'kay."

I quietly opened the door and walked down the long, dark hallway to the top of the stairs. The staircase wrapped around the side of the semi-circle wall. I followed the steps down to the first floor and crossed over to the alcove where the phone sat.

I dialed the office number. The service picked up.

"Consolidated Security."

"This is Nick Williams. Any messages?"

"Oh, my goodness, Mr. Williams! I'm so glad you called."

"Why?"

"Your house is on fire."

. . .

I let Mike do the driving. He nearly tore off the front grille of the Buick as the car bounced against the pavement while we headed down California Street at nearly sixty miles per hour. He ran the light making a left at Van Ness and did the same at Market as he turned right.

As we turned on 17th Street, I could see flashing red lights. We drove down Hartford and the scene unfolded. There were three trucks set up in front of the house. A team of firemen were holding two hoses on it. Several sets of neighbors were standing in small clusters, watching in fascinated horror, and pointing here and there.

There was something strange about the fire. Only our house was burning. Every room, it seemed to me, was on fire. It was oddly symmetrical. Neither house on either side of us was lit up. I was grateful for that.

Carter rolled down the window, leaned out, and took a deep breath while Mike looked for a place to park. Before he could even come to a stop, Carter was out the passenger door. I was sitting behind him and did the same thing. We ran across Hartford and, as we got closer, I couldn't believe what I was seeing.

We moved as close to the house as the firemen would let us. Diane came running up out of the dark. She was bundled in a robe and her thick hair was tied back in a scarf. Pam was was right behind her and was wearing a white t-shirt and dungarees. Standing next to Pam was Evelyn Key, our good friend who lived on the other side of Pam and Diane. She was wrapped in a green kimono.

"Oh, Nick. I can't believe it." That was Diane. She hugged me and I tried to hug her back but I couldn't take my eyes off what was happening. She seemed to understand and stepped back.

I put my hand in Carter's and he squeezed it. "Do you smell that?" he asked. He leaned down so I could hear. The sound of the blaze combined with the sound of the hoses was almost deafening.

All I could smell was smoke. But Carter had a keen sense of smell. It was one of the things that made him such a good arson investigator. I replied, "No."

Into my ear, he said, "Gasoline." He pointed up at the house. "Look at how every room is on fire at the same time. Someone broke in and dowsed the place, no question."

Mike walked up behind me and put his hand on my shoulder. I reached up and touched it. Carter's old fire captain strolled over, shaking his head and looking worried. Mike pulled his hand back.

Yelling to be heard, the captain said, "Sorry about this, Jones. You can see and smell what happened. Any ideas?"

Carter nodded. "Thanks, Captain. I know exactly who did it."

Mike put his hand on Carter's shoulder, leaned in, and said, "Don't." Or, at least, that's what I think he said. I couldn't hear clearly.

The captain looked at Carter. "Who?"

Carter shook his head and didn't say anything.

Mike looked at the captain and said, "We'll take it up with the police. In fact..." He turned and walked over to Evelyn. After he said something to her, she nodded and they walked down to her house. I guessed he was going to call Lieutenant Holland.

. . .

About twenty minutes later, most of the blaze was extinguished but the firemen were still pouring water over the house to cool it down. I watched and realized that I'd never once seen Carter do this kind of work in the first five years we were together. He'd been a fireman for fourteen years in total when he was fired. Although he was wisely letting the other firemen do their job, I could see that he was tensed up and having to hold himself back from grabbing the hose and jumping in.

As I was watching him silhouetted against the firetruck, Marnie walked up. She looked like she had gotten dressed in a hurry and then run over. She lived three blocks away on Collingwood.

I pulled her away from the house and down closer to Evelyn's so we wouldn't have to yell over the sound of the two fire hoses.

"Hi, doll."

"Oh, Nick." She hugged me and I hugged her back.

"Who called you?" I asked.

"One of the ladies over here. Then I called mother. They'll be over as soon as they can."

I nodded. We had grabbed Mike and run out of the house without waking anyone else up.

I was in shock. I didn't know what to say. I looked down at my clothes and realized this and a handful of other things in the car and in the house on Sacramento were all that I had left. It didn't matter but, then again, it did.

. . .

About the time my father pulled up in his new Cadillac, Lieutenant Holland was also arriving in his own car, a DeSoto. He looked annoyed to be roused out of bed again. I agreed with him. I hadn't had a good night's sleep in a couple of days.

My father walked up and stood next to me for a moment. Putting his hand on my shoulder, he said, "I'm sorry, Nicholas." I nodded and let him hug me. For some reason, I couldn't feel it. But I went through the motions.

He walked off in search of Carter as Lettie came up. "Dear boy. I'm sorry about this." She put her hand on my arm, stood with me for a moment, and then walked away. She seemed to understand I wasn't all there.

Lieutenant Holland ambled over. "Tough break, Williams. Looks like a total loss."

I nodded.

"I'm glad you weren't here."

That seemed to snap something inside of me. "I don't know, Lieutenant." I blinked a few times feeling the emotions that were finally rising to the surface. I wiped my face with the back of my hand and said, "If we'd been here, this wouldn't have happened. If we hadn't been too cowardly to stand our ground, we'd have still have a home."

I had turned to look at the house as I was talking. The lieutenant came around and got in my face. He grabbed my shoulders and shook me. It wasn't rough but it wasn't gentle. "Snap out of it, Nick. You'd both be dead if you'd been here. There's only so much you can do. You hear me?"

It was an oddly tender moment. He was obviously concerned about me. Not just my role in his case, but me. I stood there and looked at him for a moment, wondering about him and what he'd said. He looked back at me, searching my eyes. Once he was satisfied that he'd seen what he was looking for, he released my shoulders and asked, "Is Jones here?"

I nodded and pointed to where Carter stood next to one of the engines.

The lieutenant smiled at me and said, "Like I said, I'm glad you weren't here." With that, he walked away.

. . .

The lieutenant was right. It was a total loss. As the sun rose, that much was obvious. The two houses on either side had minor damage but it was mostly cosmetic.

The main structure of the house was intact but the interior was gutted. The windows were all blown out. The captain said that was from the heat.

The trucks left just before dawn. We'd thanked each of the firemen personally before they left. Station 3, where Carter used to work, had been called out on the third alarm. It was nice to see Carter's old work buddies being so sympathetic. A few of them even stopped and spoke with me.

The captain told Carter that he was welcome to join the arson team later in the afternoon. As he was leaving, the captain said to me, "I'm sorry for your loss here, Mr. Williams. It's hard to see one of our own have to deal with a fire."

I said, "Thank you, Captain. That means a lot. And thanks for asking Carter to join the investigation."

The captain shook his head. "He's the best I've ever seen. That nose of his." I smiled wanly and nodded.

"Well, it's too bad that the City lost a valuable man."

I said, "Yeah."

He touched his hat, walked over to the engine, and jumped on as it pulled away.

. . .

We were all at the dining table having breakfast when the doorbell rang. Henry and Robert had slept through the ordeal which they were both miffed about. When Henry had complained about that, I had simply said, "Count your blessings," because I was dead tired.

Zelda, the wonderful housekeeper who'd worked for my father since just after my mother had died, walked into the dining room. She handed me a Western Union telegram.

I said, "Thanks." She nodded, smiled, and walked into the kitchen.

I opened the envelope and read the message. Oddly enough, it was from Jeffery and it said, "Sorry about house. Assuming right address. Let me know if help needed." I was too tired to think about what this meant. I handed it over to Carter and stood up. I looked around the table and said, "I'm going to bed." And I did.

. . .

It was dark when I woke up. I was alone in the big bed in the big room and felt deeply alone for the first time in a long time. I wondered where Carter was. And, as I lay there and thought about the house, I began to cry.

I wasn't crying for the things. Those could be replaced. I was crying for everything. My sister Janet, who'd died in the hospital right in front of Carter and me. My mother, who I barely knew. Mack, my friend who sailed away and never came back. Jeffery, my lover who wasn't dead but might as well have been. Nacho, the police captain in Mexico who'd asked Carter for a kiss before he died in my arms. Even poor Mr. Kopek, Ike's old man, who'd had a heart attack after trying to kill a man and died on the floor of the hospital.

The more I remembered, the more I cried. And this wasn't just a few tears. This was sobbing and heaving. The kind that leaves you gasping for breath. The kind that makes you wonder whether it will ever end. The kind that seems like it's going to engulf you and swallow you whole.

Eventually, though, the tears did stop and everything was quiet. I lay in bed and listened for the sounds of the house and there were none. No voices from downstairs were being echoed by the marble floor in front of the staircase like I remembered from years ago. No water was running telling me that dinner or lunch or breakfast was being prepared. No footsteps were coming down the hall to check on me, to sit down next to me, to hold me, to rock me.

No one was there.

I was all alone in this big pile of rocks and everyone was gone. It was eerie. I couldn't remember a time when that house hadn't been full of sound, even in the worst times. Someone, at least, was always working to clean, to polish, to peal, to cook.

Even during the long evening when the radio was forbidden and my father sat in his office, smoking his cigar, and doing nothing but staring into space, I had never felt this alone.

Even when Janet and I would play some game she made up, in her room and in total silence to keep from getting into trouble, someone was walking around tending to the fires.

Even when I lay in my bed and looked out the

window at the stars or the fog, I could hear the scrape of shoe leather from, the passersby on Sacramento or the reassuring clang of a bell on a passing cable car over on California.

The house, my home, had never been quiet like it was right then.

The emptiness of that thought threatened to overwhelm me, but I pushed it away. I was tired of being sad and lonely. I'd never had much patience for the deep-running emotions. It just wasn't in my nature.

I took a deep breath and thought about a cigarette, but that seemed like too much trouble. I wondered what time it was, but I didn't care enough to look at my watch. I turned over on my stomach, and fell back to sleep.

. . .

The next time I woke up, Carter was in bed next to me. He was sitting up and reading more of the history book that he'd given my father.

"Hi there," I said, feeling groggy.

Carter closed the book, slid down in the bed, and turned to face me.

I touched his face. There was a trace of soot right at his hairline. I licked my finger, reached over, and rubbed it off. "Did you go look at the house with the arson team?"

He nodded. As he did, I watched a tear roll out of his left eye and onto the light green sheet that covered the mattress. I kissed him very gently on the lips and put my hand under his chin. Another tear fell onto the sheet. And then another.

I smiled and motioned at him. He turned to face the other direction. I wanted to pull him in close, but it was hard to embrace Carter. He was so much wider than me. So, I slipped my arm under his and squeezed on his chest. His neck was in my face and I kissed it lightly while tasting the remnants of soot and sweat. In the light of the chrome lamp, I held him while he cried and sobbed just as I had done earlier, whenever that was. I kept whispering, "Sweet baby," over and over again. I had no idea why.

. . .

I woke up as the light of dawn began to make its way through the big windows of the bedroom. We were in exactly the same position we'd been when we'd fallen asleep. Carter was in front of me. I had my left arm under his and wrapped around his chest. He was holding my hand in his. My face was resting on his neck. I had slept on my right arm and, as I moved, I could feel the pins and needles in my hand.

I quietly pulled my hand out of his, got out of bed, and reached for my trousers and shirt. They both smelled smoky but I didn't really care. I pulled them on and walked out into the hallway and next door to the bathroom.

As I stood there relieving myself, I could remember everything that had happened but I didn't feel the grief of it. It was as if something about it had lightened up. I didn't know how to think about what I was feeling. I just felt cleansed.

I couldn't remember crying like that since I had been a small child. And, to be honest, it felt good. It was like something very old and very decrepit had left me. I felt lighter, somehow. Not happier. Just not as oppressed.

I pulled the chain on the toilet and listened to the pipes groan slightly. Even so, I was amazed that the plumbing up on the third floor was still functional.

I walked over to the mirror and looked at myself. My

hair was all over the place. I hadn't washed my face from earlier and there was soot and grime all over it. I looked at my chocolate milk eyes and wondered, for the thousandth time, what it would be like if they were green like Henry's.

My dimple was still there, however. I could remember my mother saying, at some time or another, that if I didn't behave, my dimple would disappear. So, every time I looked in the mirror, the first thing I looked for was to see whether it was still there. And, it was.

I heard a quiet knock on the door. "Nick?" It was Carter.

I opened the door and watched as my husband, in just his BVDs, ran the eight or so feet to the toilet. As he relieved himself, I closed the door and locked it. Turning to the bathtub, I started running the hot and cold water to see what would happen. There was some more groaning, and the first bit of water was rusty, but it came out and the hot water was hotter than I expected. I pulled the shower curtain into place and pulled the plug on the shower. More slight groaning, but it worked.

I dropped my clothes in a pile and stepped into the large tub. It was not the big iron Edwardian claw-foot that we'd had in our house when we bought it. In keeping with the rest of the bathroom, with its square chrome fixtures, this was rectangular and had the usual Art Deco styling.

Carter dropped his BVDs and stepped in behind me. As usual, he reached over my head and moved the shower head up to aim it at his face. That's when we discovered that time had been passing on the third floor, even though it seemed otherwise. The shower head broke off and we both started laughing and didn't stop for a while.

Chapter 7

Union Square
Saturday, June 19, 1954
Around 2 in the afternoon

We sat in the park across from the I. Magnin store and enjoyed the warm sunshine. My coat was slung over Carter's. We both had our sleeves rolled up. I was fanning myself with my hat.

A man selling ice cream from a cart moved in our general direction. I elbowed Carter and he stood up, walked over, got us each an Eskimo Pie, and returned with a pile of paper napkins. Once those were gone, I stood up and stretched.

The park was full of busy shoppers on their way from one store to another. There was also a handful of folks like us, just sitting on the benches taking in the warmth of the day. But there didn't appear to be anyone out of place. As far as we could tell, no one was tailing us.

I looked around for a quick moment and then down at Carter. I said, "I think we have enough clothes to last a couple of weeks, don't you?"

He nodded and smiled. Looking off in the distance, he said, "I never knew shopping was this much work."

I reached over for my coat. "Me, neither. Let's go, Chief."

He stood up, looked around casually, and grabbed his coat. As he swung it over his shoulder, I quietly asked, "See anyone?"

"Nope. Cable car?"

I nodded and we walked over to Powell Street to grab the next one going up the hill.

. . .

We jumped off at California Street. We made our way to my father's house by walking west along California and then crossing through Huntington Park. Instead of going through the front door, we walked around to the side and knocked on the kitchen door.

The cook, Mrs. Young, answered. As we walked up the steps into the little entryway, she smiled and asked, "Find anything you liked?"

As we walked in, I said, "Carter said it best. Shopping is hard work."

She smiled and asked, "It is, at that. Would either of you like a sandwich?"

I said, "Not me."

Carter said, "I'm fine, thanks."

Nodding and leading the way into the kitchen, she said, "I've been told to expect a large party tonight. We'll be having a buffet in the dining room and then it's seat yourself."

I asked, "A party?"

Mrs. Young was just past 50 and had a stout but solid

figure. She'd come to the house with Zelda, so she'd been around for quite a while. She was a sweet woman but not too bright. She was the only person, other than Zelda, that I'd had any patience for when I was a teenager. I had never heard if there ever was a Mr. Young. She'd been single when she came to work for my father and had never dated, as far as I knew.

As soon as I asked, I wished I hadn't said anything. She put her hand on her mouth and said, "Oh, Mr. Nick, I think it was to be a surprise."

Carter said, "That's fine, Mrs. Young. We won't give it away."

Looking up at him, she smiled. "Thank you, Mr. Carter. I'd appreciate that."

As we walked through the large kitchen, I could see that there were a couple of girls who were helping out. They had probably been hired for the day. I looked around and asked, "Are deviled eggs on the menu?"

Mrs. Young looked up, panicked. "We'll be sure to make some."

I smiled and said, "Don't worry. Our neighbor Diane will probably be bringing a platter or two of them. I wanted to mention it because they're the best you've ever had so be sure to leave some for the rest of us."

Mrs. Young laughed while the two girls giggled.

. . .

As we were passing through the sitting room, Mike was coming down the stairs.

"Feeling better, Nick?"

I nodded. "Yeah. What's the latest?"

Mike said, "Come upstairs with me. I was hoping I'd see you. I wanna fill you in."

We walked with him up to the third floor. He was camped out in the Sapphire Room and it was definitely blue in there. The layout and all the furniture was exactly the same as our room. Everything was blue instead of green. I had a vague memory that this room had been used for sewing and making clothes before my mother had renovated everything.

Mike sat down on the bed while Carter and I pulled over two plush sapphire chairs.

"What's up?" Carter asked.

"I don't know what happened to Lieutenant Holland, but now he's my best friend. I guess he's grateful I called him about the fire since Eureka Valley is in the Mission District. But there's something else going on with him and I don't know what it is."

I nodded. Carter asked, "Do you trust him?"

Mike made a face. "Yes and no. I trust him to do what he says he's gonna do but there's something fishy there. I can't put my finger on it."

"What else?" I asked.

"Holland told me they canvassed your block of Hartford and no one saw anything."

I looked at Carter. "What time did the fire get called in?"

He replied, "The call came in around 2 in the morning."

Mike said, "Yeah, but that Lysander Blythe who lives on the south side of you told the cops that he was sure he heard breaking glass around 1:30."

"Did he call that in?"

Mike shook his head. "How well do you know them?"

"Lysander and Vivienne? Just to talk to. They moved in around January of last year. Quiet couple. He writes for a living. Never read anything by him."

Mike exchanged looks with Carter.

"What?" I asked.

Carter said, "You really are the worst when it comes

to neighbors, Nick. Lysander Blythe is one of the biggest playwrights in the country. Right now one of his plays is sold out for months on Broadway."

"Really?" I asked. "Is it a musical?"

Carter shook his head. "No. It's Southern Gothic. It's called *The Voice She Heard*."

I shrugged. "That's why. You know I only like musicals. And I hate stories about oversexed southern women. What's this have to do with anything? And why don't they live in New York?"

Mike said, "They did. But they left. Something about trouble with one of the actresses."

Carter put in, "Not just any actress. The star of the show. Kim Taylor. And that isn't the first time it's happened."

"Again," I asked a little impatiently, "Why Eureka Valley and how does this involve us?"

Mike leaned over. "Blythe is writing a new play. There was a thing about it in Herb Caen last week." He was a snappy, witty daily columnist who once had a radio show back in the 30s that Mrs. Young used to love to listen to. He was now published by the *Examiner*.

"So?"

Carter laughed and said to Mike. "He really doesn't read the papers anymore. And I hadn't gotten around to telling him with all the excitement going on."

"Goddam it, you two! What the hell is going on?"

Mike said, "The play is about you. Herb Caen said the working title was *Notorious Nick*. Of course, you could sue him if he used that title."

I just rolled my eyes. "So, you're saying that Elliott moved in next door in order to write a play about me?"

Mike shook his head. "No. I went over and talked to the guy myself."

Carter sat back. "Does he know who you are in

relation to Nick?"

Mike shrugged. "I might be another cop, for all he knows."

I said, "Damn it, Mike!"

He put his hand out. "I know. Look. Here's the story. They came out west but didn't want to live the Park Avenue life on Nob Hill so they bought a nice cozy bungalow and, it turns out, happened to buy right next to you. I don't know when he figured out who you were but, once he did, that got the creative juices flowing."

"Why would he set the fire?" I asked.

Mike replied with a confused look. "Who said anything about that?"

"This whole little trip down the gay white way started when I asked what time the fire started."

"Right." He shrugged apologetically. "So, he was sitting at his typewriter and heard breaking glass. I got him to admit that he didn't call the cops because he wanted to see what might happen. He thought it was a burglary or something. Said he figured you and Carter could handle things. Didn't know you weren't there. Of course, once the fire was going, he realized the mistake he'd made and called it in. And that was around 2."

I just shook my head. "For crying out loud, what an idiot."

Carter laughed. "Yeah." Looking at Mike, he asked, "You gonna tell Holland all about what you found out?"

Mike pressed his lips together and said, "Yeah. Have to."

I looked up at him. "Have you figured out how you're gonna explain the way you got your foot in the door?"

Mike shrugged. "Truth is, that's small potatoes compared to the big news I have for him."

"What?" I asked.

"Sam says the fire wasn't set by Abati or any of his

gang."

Carter and I exchanged looks. He asked, "Sam? How does he know?"

Mike grinned at me and yanked on his tie to loosen it. "What we didn't know about Sam is a whole hell of a lot. He has mob connections."

I'm pretty sure my mouth dropped open.

"What connections?" That was Carter. He was immediately suspicious.

"Sam used to run around with some of the muscle. He says that Sugar Joe's is a place where some of the beefier wiseguys do their weights and boxing." Sugar Joe's was a gymnasium on Mission that Carter used to frequent. That was also where Ike first met Sam the year before. "Sam told me this group of muscle was known as 'The Frutti Tutti.' They're all queer. And, all the guys are older. They're Sam's age. They date back to Lanza, when he was running things."

Carter whistled. "Queer mob muscle."

Mike nodded and continued, "A couple have retired to Mexico. The other one still works for the mob. Sam never did any jobs with these guys, but he knows them. Anyway, he made some inquiries yesterday and, come to find out, Abati doesn't have a hit out on any of us. From what he can figure out, rubbing out Johnny Russell was an inside job."

Carter asked, "Inside job? What does that mean?"

Mike replied, "It means it was only about the mob. Russell didn't deliver on something he promised. That it happened at your building, Nick, is a coincidence. Just happened to be a convenient place to do the job and what better place to dump the body, right?"

I frowned. "Right." There was something off about this. "Seems sloppy for the mob, though."

Mike cocked his head and looked at me for a

moment. Before he could say anything, Carter asked, "So, who called Henry and who torched our house?"

Mike pressed his lips together. "That's the sixty-four dollar question, ain't it?"

I asked, "When are you gonna report all this to Holland?"

"I was headed over to Central when I ran into you guys."

Carter leaned in and asked, "Mike, do you have any suspicion at all about who it might have been? Any guesses?"

Mike shook his head. "None. There's plenty of people in this town who don't like Nick but I can't see any of them hiring a firebug."

Carter looked thoughtful. "This wasn't a firebug. Whoever did it was a pro. Or knew what he was doing."

Mike said, "Yeah. It was too clean."

Carter nodded and said, "We both kept our eyes opened when we went down to Union Square and neither of us saw anyone tailing us. This explains that." He crossed his arms and leaned back. "Have you told Henry, yet?"

"Whoa." Mike put up his hands like a cop directing traffic.

"What?" I asked.

"I have a bone to pick with you guys."

"What?" That was Carter.

"You should've called Andy and Dawson to go with you."

I shrugged.

Carter looked at me and then back at Mike. He nodded. "You're right, Mike. We should have." He looked at me again.

I shrugged again.

Mike looked put out. "I want you to take this

seriously. One of these days your lone wolf move could get you killed."

I rolled my eyes. He was right but my dander was up and I didn't want to admit it. I changed the subject. "So, what about Henry?"

Mike shook his head. "At least listen to Carter."

Carter punched me playfully in the arm. "Yeah. Listen to your husband. Pipsqueak."

Mike grinned, "Small fry."

"For cryin' out loud, you two." I sighed. "Now. Henry. Did you tell him?"

Mike smirked and said, "I did. He moved back over to Robert's place. They'll be here for the party tonight."

"What about you?" I asked.

"Ray's gonna take me home after the party."

I said, "In spite of everything, thanks for taking such good care of us, Mike."

Carter nodded, reached over, and squeezed Mike's arm. "Yeah. Thanks."

Mike smiled. "That's what we do at Consolidated Security."

Chapter 8

1198 Sacramento Street
Saturday, June 19, 1954
Later in the afternoon

Some of what we'd bought at Union Square had already been delivered by the time we got back to the house. We were in our room unpacking the boxes and putting things away in the wardrobe and the bureau when someone knocked on the door.

Carter said, "Come on in."

"Hello." It was my father.

"How are you?" I asked.

"Fine, fine." He pulled on his pipe and looked around. "You get what you were looking for?"

I nodded as I closed the drawer in the bureau that I'd been packing with brand-new garters and rolled-up socks. "Enough to get started."

"Good, good." He seemed to want to say something. So, I turned around, leaned against the bureau, and waited.

"I have something I want to say to you both."

Carter had been hanging up shirts in the wardrobe. He stopped what he was doing and turned around.

"What is it?" I asked.

"Lettie and I wanted to do this before we got married but it didn't make sense then."

We both waited.

"You see, neither of us wants to live here." He fiddled with his pipe as he said this.

I was surprised. I looked over at Carter who had crossed his arms and was avoiding my gaze.

"And, since you're in need of a home, we'd like for you to move in."

I didn't know what to say, so I asked the obvious question, "Where will you two go?"

"Not far. I've already rented an apartment on the fourth floor of 1055 California." That was the building across the street from the Pacific Union Club. I could see it from the window of the room we were in. "It's already been remodeled and furnished. I was going to sub-lease it for the time being, but..." He looked at his pipe. "We can move in a week."

"Are you sure about this?" asked Carter. His voice was doubtful. But it was also hopeful, which surprised me even more than what my father was saying.

My father nodded. Looking at me, he said, "I want you two to think about it. The upkeep on a house like this isn't the same as a bungalow in Eureka Valley." He looked down at the emerald green carpeting and kicked at it with his shoe, something I'd never seen him do before. "But you know that."

I was dumbfounded. This solved all sorts of problems. But, I didn't want to leave Eureka Valley with its ladies who play mah-jong and its families who took long strolls on Sunday after Mass. I would miss being neighbors with Pam and Diane. Not to mention Evelyn down the street and Marnie a few blocks away. I liked the neighborhood. It was quaint and sweet. And it's where we lived.

I took a deep breath and said, "We'll talk about it and let you know."

My father said, "Fair enough."

As he turned to leave, one important thought crossed my mind. "What about Zelda?"

My father stopped and turned back. His eyes were crinkled in amusement. "Let's just say that Lettie tolerates Zelda. As long as they're willing, Zelda and the other staff come with the house. Lettie will be more than happy to hire her own housekeeper." He looked at Carter and then at me. "What about your housekeeper?"

"Mrs. Kopek," I said.

Carter said, "That's something we have to consider. Would there be room for her here?"

I said, "No, but we'll figure something out." Something else crossed my mind. "What about the mountain?"

This made my father laugh. "Oh, I'll take all my treasures with me. But, I updated the safe earlier this year because I knew you would want your own mountain."

Carter laughed. "He already has one."

"Oh?"

"Or do we?" I looked at Carter.

He nodded. "The Chicago Fireproof Safe Company has that name for a reason. I couldn't open it, but it's still there."

. . .

Carter's eyes were dancing as he looked at me. He waited a decent amount of time for my father to be gone and out of earshot. He then walked over with a big grin on his face. He lifted me up under my arms and kissed me soundly on the lips. I laughed as he put his hand under my ass and tossed me over his shoulder. He let out a resounding yelp, slapped me on the rear, and threw me on the bed.

I lay there, immobile and stunned. My first thought was how surprised I was that he was strong enough to do that. I weighed around 150 and that was no mean feat.

My second thought was that I would never have expected Carter Woodrow Wilson Jones, a nice boy from Albany, Georgia, to react this way. But then I remembered how, back in '49, he'd prodded me for months to buy a house in the first place. He even found the place himself. And then threatened to take out a mortgage and split it with me while knowing I could have easily bought a hundred such houses without too much trouble. Suddenly several things made sense.

"You sneaky-ass bastard," were the first words that came out of my mouth.

He was stripping off his clothes and had a wild look on his face. "What?" he asked with his big grin.

"How long have you been working on this?"

"Since the day I picked your father up and dropped him on his bony little ass." By now he was down to his garters and socks, but he didn't bother with those and got right to the matter at hand.

. . .

We were stretched out in bed sharing a Camel between us when I finally asked, "How long have you been thinking about this? Tell me the truth, Carter."

He handed me the cigarette and said, "It's just what I said. Ever since your sister's funeral."

"But why?"

"Because the old man told me then that he didn't want to live here anymore. Too many bad memories."

He put his hand out and I gave him the cigarette.

"I can understand that sentiment."

Carter sat up and looked over at me. "You don't want to leave Eureka Valley, do you?"

I sighed. "No. But I can't imagine building a new house or trying to repair that one." I looked around the room. It really was beautiful. It could've easily been in a museum. Maybe that was the problem. For me, at least. "It's so cold here. Even with Lettie here, it's still cold."

Carter looked at me deeply. "Have you noticed that she hasn't done any decorating of her own? She hasn't even moved any furniture."

"What about the office?"

"Your old man did that after the wedding."

"How do you know that?"

"I helped him with some of it."

I sat up and crossed my legs. "What?"

"Sure. I was the one who suggested removing the Persian rug. Marnie and I found the guys who restored the wood floor."

"Damn it, Carter. You're in up to your eyeballs on this, aren't you?"

"On what?" He grinned that lopsided grin he could get every now and then.

"On getting us moved in here."

He shook his head, reached over to the side table, and stubbed out the last of the cigarette.

"No. I was just helping out your father. He's never said anything to me about *moving* since last year." I noticed he put a special emphasis on the word "moving." I wondered what that meant.

"Look, Nick. It's cold here because a bitter old man had been living here by himself for... How long?"

"Nine years."

"He needs to move on. And she definitely deserves her own home. And they don't need a big pile of rocks."

I laughed at his use of my phrase. "You're right about all that. He could just sell, though."

"For God's sake Nick, he's still a Williams. He may be improving with age but he's still got that Welsh mettle that you Williams men all have."

"Welsh mettle?"

"That's Mike's phrase, not mine. But it's true."

I grabbed his hand, pulled it to my face, and kissed the back of it.

"What's that for?"

I started to reply but then stopped. It was as if the answer to this question of whether to move in and take over was suddenly settled. I kissed his hand again. He came up close and embraced me from behind, stretching his legs around mine. "Don't you feel it?" I asked.

"Feel what?" He kissed the back of my neck.

"How romantic we are when we're here together."

"We've been here two nights. What are you talking about?"

I was getting that same feeling I'd had when the idea to start Consolidated Security had come over me. It was a curious mix of anticipation of something wonderful and a deep feeling of the rightness of everything.

"We belong here, Carter."

He laughed and kissed my neck again. I leaned back and let him hold the weight of me.

"We do, Nick."

"No, I don't mean like that. I mean, *we belong here.*

94

Can't you feel it?"

Carter was quiet for a moment. I could feel his heart beating as I leaned against his chest. I looked out the window as the light began to dim. I could see fog moving across the sky.

Whispering in my ear, he said, "Remember at Christmas?"

"I do. That's what I mean. I've thought a lot about that afternoon in my old bedroom. I thought it was just that day. All that happened."

"That could be the same thing now. Our lives have just burned down to the ground, after all."

"Yeah." I thought for another moment, reaching for the right words. "The house might be cold. But, when I'm here with you, right now, I'm alive and warm."

He reached one hand around my chest and rubbed my shoulder with the other. "I love you, Nicholas Williams."

. . .

Once we were all cleaned up, we walked down to the second floor. Holding Carter's hand, I knocked on my father's bedroom door.

Lettie opened it and said, "Come in, boys."

We followed her in. I hadn't been in that room in a very long time but it looked exactly the same as I remembered. A gigantic four-poster bed was against one wall. Across from it was a large fireplace, almost as large as the one downstairs. Two tall windows flanked the mantle. A row of tall windows looked down over Sacramento. Heavy drapes covered all but one of them, which was open. The fog was getting thicker by the moment.

My father was sitting in a large leather chair next to the fireplace which had a small fire burning in it, even though it was June. That explained the open window.

Lettie said, "Have a seat," and pointed to the old brown leather Chesterfield opposite of where my father was sitting. We did so as she primly sat on the arm of my father's chair.

Looking down at his pipe, my father said, "Well?"

I replied, "We'll do it."

Lettie looked at me with a twinkle in her eye. I knew I had just made her very happy. Carter was right. My father would never have sold this house.

He looked up at Carter. "And you agree?"

Carter nodded.

I said, "Don't you try to fool me, old man."

Lettie smiled briefly and then looked appropriately shocked.

My father sat up, mildly irritated, and said, "What the blazes are you talking about, Nicholas?"

"I know a scheme when I see one. If I didn't know the three of you better, I'd say that you set the fire yourselves."

Carter exclaimed, "What the hell, Nick?"

"Weren't you just lecturing me about Welsh mettle?"

My father smiled in spite of himself and then cleared his throat. "You can't just walk in here and make accusations like that."

"It's not an accusation. And don't get worked up about it." I smiled and let myself be myself. "It's not what I would have imagined in a thousand years, but I think it's a damn fine scheme, myself."

My father smiled and said, "What were you going to do with the house after... You know."

"Sell it."

Lettie looked truly shocked. "You wouldn't have, though, would you?"

I shook my head. "Not now. Not for all the tea in

China. I can't believe it, but I'm finally fucking coming home."

Everyone laughed and then Lettie added, "Please be more careful of your language, Nicholas."

. . .

Before everyone arrived for the party, Carter and I sat down with Zelda in my father's office. After we explained what was going to happen, I got down to brass tacks. "Would you like to stay on?"

She looked at both of us for a long moment and then shook her head. "I know you are both fine gentlemen but I don't think I could live under the same roof knowing what would be going on in your father's bedroom."

I smiled and sat back. "Thanks for your candor, Zelda. It won't be the same without you and I'll miss you."

She rose briskly. "Will you be talking with the rest of the staff?"

We both stood up. Carter said, "Yes. But we wanted to talk with you first."

She smiled and said, "I appreciate that, Mr. Jones."

I said, "And, I'll be giving you a year's pay in severance. You'll have it on Friday. That will be your last day unless you think you need to go sooner."

She looked at me in surprise. "A year?"

I nodded. "It's probably not enough considering all you've done here."

She looked at me for a long moment. Finally, she smiled in reply. "Friday will be fine."

. . .

We went to each member of the staff and told them about the changes. We also told them that they should expect visible signs of affection between us and that we understood if they couldn't stay under those conditions. For better or for worse, they all quit.

. . .

I never heard who came up with the idea for a party but, since Marnie took care of things, it was a great evening.

Although my father had a substantial wine cellar, Pam brought a couple of gallons of the red wine she got from somewhere in Napa. I preferred hers to any that I'd ever tasted elsewhere. She still couldn't remember the name of the winery, though.

Diane brought two platters of her deviled eggs. They were the hit of the party, as always.

When Mrs. Kopek, our housekeeper, had arrived with Sam and Ike, she was a little weepy over our losing the house in the fire. We pulled her into my father's office and asked her if she would consider staying on and working for us here. We told her we would have to hire some new staff. She looked around the room and said, "Fine. I stay. You let me hire. No worry for you."

I nodded and said, "That would a big relief. Thank you, Mrs. Kopek."

"This live-in?"

I nodded. "Yes. It's a big job."

"Fine. I have friend you give my apartment to. Same as before. No rent. She just escape from Czechoslovakia. Good girl."

I nodded again. "That's fine, Mrs. Kopek. Talk to Robert about it."

She nodded and looked around again. Standing up, she walked over to my father's desk. "Furniture stay?"

I shrugged. "I don't know."

"You keep this. It belong here. You know?"

Carter said, "Of course, it stays here."

I turned and asked, "Have you already seen the new apartment?"

Carter turned a little red and replied, "Well, yeah."

I just shook my head and whispered, "You sneaky bastard."

. . .

Once we'd all eaten, Carter walked around the house and gathered everyone into the big sitting room. He had decided to call it the great room and I decided he was right. That was a much better name for it.

One of the kitchen helpers had set up bottles of French champagne and a tray of coupe glasses. Carter and I walked around and poured for everyone. Once all the glasses were topped up, Carter said, "We have a big announcement to make and I'm glad you're all here for it."

I surveyed the room. All of our friends were there. Pam and Diane. Henry and Robert. Mike and Ray. Ben and Carlo. Andy, who worked with us and grew up with Carter and Henry in Georgia, and his squeeze Dawson, who also worked with us. Evelyn and her new girlfriend Mary. Sam and Ike. Ralph, my amazing travel agent, and his gal pal Roxie. Marnie had even called Johnny, my real estate agent and his lover Rob, who was an interior designer.

Marnie had brought her new boyfriend, a nice guy by the name of Alex. This was the first time she had introduced him to any of her family or friends. I felt sorry for the guy. It was an unusual group and a lot to take in at once. But he smiled and nodded and laughed his way through it. And the way he looked at Marnie when she didn't know he was watching her told me it was love.

My father and Lettie stood together near the double doors that led out into a small garden behind the house. Carter and I were next to the fireplace.

Carter looked around the room and said, "The past couple of days have been really hard for everyone. I want to thank Dr. and Mrs. Williams for taking us in."

My father raised his glass in response and Lettie beamed.

"As many of you know, I was the one who finally convinced Nick to get off his ass back in 1949 and spend some of his loot on our wonderful little bungalow on Hartford Street."

This brought some guffaws. I noticed that Alex was befuddled. Marnie leaned up and whispered something to him. He just smiled at her as she did.

"Today, Dr. Williams came to Nick and me and asked us to help him with a problem he had. Seems like Mrs. Williams wants to make a home of her own and I know the feeling. For some reason, it's hard to get these Williams men to move."

There were several chuckles, particularly from Mike, who winked at me.

Carter walked over and put his arm around me. "So, we said we'd help him out. On Friday, they're moving across the park into an apartment. And we're moving in here."

There were a few gasps and then several people began to offer their congratulations. Carter lifted his glass and said, "So, my toast is to this old pile of rocks." Everyone, even my father, laughed. "Long may she stand!"

Chapter 9

We left Sacramento Street just as dawn was breaking the next morning. It was cool but clear. The thick fog from the day before was gone.

We parked in front of Pam and Diane's house. There was no place to park in our driveway as it was covered in debris.

A portion of the roof had collapsed in on itself at some point since Friday morning. What was left of the front door was resting at an angle, holding on to the frame by one hinge. There was a scorched hole in the front porch right in front of the door. Carter pointed at that and said, "He probably poured the last bit of gasoline right there."

"Why didn't the whole porch disintegrate?" I asked.

"It was probably only a few drops. I'll know more

101

once we can get in on Monday and take more of a look around."

Right then, I heard Pam call out, "Coffee, anyone?"

We walked up the steps of their porch and followed Pam inside. We'd been to their house a number of times. It was a little larger than ours and was crammed and jammed with furniture of all styles. There was an Art Deco chair with a vibrant arrow pattern on it next to a blood red Queen Anne settee. All the furniture was comfortable. That was the main criteria and I liked that.

We followed Pam into the kitchen where we found Diane in her robe with her thick hair tied back in a scarf, much as she'd looked on Friday morning.

She said, "Good morning," and yawned.

Pam sat down at the kitchen table and looked up. "I can't believe you're leaving us."

Diane said, "Hush, Pam. Sit down, you two." We did so as she passed out coffee mugs.

I said, "I can't believe it either but I also can't imagine re-building that house and then living in it. Besides, did you see Lettie's face last night when Carter made his toast? My father won't sell and she really wants out of there."

As she moved around the table, pouring coffee for each of us, Diane asked, "What about all the people who work for them?"

Carter replied, "They all quit."

Pam shook her head. "Can't take working for them queers, huh?"

I nodded. "That's about it. They were all very polite about it."

"Plus, he gave them all a year's severance," Carter added.

Diane put the percolator back on the stove and sat

down. "That seems like a lot, Nick."

I said, "I'm not sure it's enough considering what they had to put up with all these years."

Carter said, "Anyway, we have Mrs. Kopek on the job. She'll have the place in shape in no time."

Diane asked, "Will you have to hire new people?"

I said, "Yeah. But she's gonna take care of it."

Right then, their two very annoying dogs began to yap outside the back door. Pam got up, opened the door, and the two terrors went straight for Carter, who scooped them up in his lap and began to weave his magical spells on them.

. . .

Using their back door, we made our way into the wreckage of our back garden. There were pieces of charred wood all over the grass.

Carter unlocked the basement door and pulled it open after kicking a few shingles out of the way. The basement was pretty much intact although there was water standing everywhere. As we walked around in the puddles, I said, "I guess it's a good thing you decided you didn't want a gymnasium built down here." That had been one of my Christmas gifts for Carter.

He chuckled. "What about the ring your father gave you?"

"It's always in my pocket. What about the cuff links?"

"I was wearing them."

I'd found a pair of platinum and sapphire cuff links for Carter, also for Christmas. My father, coincidentally, had given me the matching ring. I already had a gold band that I wore that Carter had given me in Mexico. I didn't really care about my

103

father's ring other than the fact that he'd given it to me. That was the reason I carried it around even though I never wore it.

The kitchen floor above us was buckled in several places. I poked my head up the stairwell and asked, "Do you think it's safe?"

Carter came and stood next to me. Then he looked under the stairs. "Might be. I'll give it a try."

I pushed back on him. "I'm fifty pounds lighter, let me go first."

He grunted in assent as I cautiously put my foot on the first step. As I ascended, I tested each piece of wood before putting my full weight on it. When I got to the top step, I turned the knob on the door that led to the kitchen and then pushed. There was a grinding sound and I could feel the weight of whatever was in the way. I said, "There's something blocking the door."

Carter called up. "Let me see if I can move it."

I walked back down and said, "Have at it, big guy."

He grinned, walked gingerly up the stairs, and stopped at the top. He pushed hard on whatever it was and I could hear some movement but he was only able to open the door about three inches. It was enough for daylight to come through but not much else.

He came back down the stairs and wiped his hands with his handkerchief. "There's a crossbeam or two that's blocking the door."

I sighed. I'd really hoped we'd be able to poke around upstairs. We walked over to the back of the room. Carter said, "Let's see if we can get the safe open."

It had been behind the washing machine. Carter had obviously moved it the last time he was trying to open it up. We both pulled on the mechanism and were able to open the secret panel that hid the safe. I paused for a moment, remembering the combination. Once I was sure I had it, I rotated the dials until I heard the familiar click. Turning the handle, I pulled on the door to reveal the interior.

Carter's immediate response was, "What the hell?"

It was empty.

We stood there for a moment and looked at each other and then back at the safe. I reached in and felt around, thinking for a moment that maybe the inside was larger than what I remembered.

"How much was in there?" Carter asked.

I shook my head. "It was all cash. Half a million. That's all that would fit in stacks of hundreds. There was also fifty thousand in thousand-dollar bills."

Carter took off his hat and regarded it for a moment. He sighed dramatically and bit down on the brim.

"What?" I asked.

"I told you in October that if anyone found this safe that I would eat my hat. Have any salt?"

. . .

Carter was munching on some toast. As he smeared it with some apple butter, I saw him suddenly stop. I looked up at his face and there was a tear coming down his left cheek.

"What?" I softly asked.

He banged the table with his fist, which caused some commotion at the nearby tables. We were having breakfast among the tourists at the Mark Hopkins. "I don't care about the money but that bastard who torched our house destroyed the last jar of my mother's red plum jam."

"I already sent in my check to the Dougherty County Hospital Board. Your Aunt Velma told me that the next batch should be ready in a couple of weeks. She said the blossoms were thick back in the spring and how that's a good sign." We'd been receiving a case or two of Mrs. Jones's red plum jam for a few years. Her sister, Carter's Aunt Velma, would send it to us in exchange for a nice donation to the hospital. I had called Aunt Velma a few weeks earlier because I wasn't sure our little scheme would continue now that Mrs. Jones knew about it. Fortunately, she had reassured me it would. Carter and his mother had mostly reconciled the summer before after his father was murdered, but they weren't speaking to each other very often. At least they were talking, and that was an improvement.

Carter made a growling noise. "Well, when I find the man, I'm gonna kick his ass. No one, but no one, messes with my mama's red plum jam and lives to tell the tale."

I grinned at him and said, "I wouldn't want to be in those shoes."

He relaxed, smiled a little, and took a sip of coffee. He sighed and said, "I wonder how long this will keep going on?"

"What?"

"I just remembered something else that's gone."

"We'll be in our seventies, sitting on a porch in rocking chairs, saying, 'You remember that thingamabob that got burnt up in the fire?'"

Carter smiled at me. "Are you plannin' on having a southern accent by the time you're 70?"

"That's just old-timer talk."

"Will we be old timers if we're living on Mars?"

"Sure. Mars will have the best old age homes, just you wait and see." I took a drink of my coffee. "What'd you remember?"

"Your trophies."

After I'd bought a Lockheed Super Constellation the previous summer, Carter had set up what he called a "trophy wall" in our bedroom. He'd first installed a model ship that somewhat resembled *The Flirtatious Captain,* our yacht that was docked in a marina over on the bay. He'd also installed a model Constellation and, then in February, he'd added a model DC-7 when I'd bought one of those. He'd said it was better than having a trophy wall full of moose and deer heads.

I asked, "Where you gonna put the trophy wall in the new house?"

"Our office, of course."

"Our office?"

"Sure. The one with the big safe in the floor."

I nodded and said, "I see. How's that gonna work? You can't hang anything on those walls." The entire room had been designed for my grandfather. The walls and the ceiling were beautifully paneled in a number of inlaid woods. The whole room was really a work of art.

"I'll get one of those trophy cases and set it up along the wall next to the desk." For some reason, his Georgia accent was getting stronger.

I smiled. "Well, I got dibs on the desk that's already in there. You'd better start looking for one of your own."

Carter rubbed his finger along the rim of his coffee cup, which I always liked to watch, for some reason. In a thick husky voice, he said, "Oh, I will."

I laughed. "Are we really having this kind of conversation about desks and trophy cases?"

Carter smiled his slow, southern smile and replied, "You bet, son."

I looked around for the waiter and said, "I'm ready to go back, now. Right now."

Carter just stared at me.

. . .

107

Once we'd taken another shower and were getting dressed again, I said, "We need to call Mike about the money in the safe."

Carter, who was putting on his tie, nodded and said, "You go call him. I want to talk to your father about something."

I stood up and put on my coat. Then I noticed something. "Hey. You're not bending over." For once, he was using a mirror that was long enough that he could see himself without stooping. For some reason, we'd never changed out the mirror in the bedroom or the bathroom in the house on Hartford.

Carter said, "Ain't it grand? This is like..." He grinned at me. "Hell, it's like livin' on goddam Nob Hill, son."

. . .

Ray answered the phone.

"Hi, it's Nick. Is Mike around?"

"Sure." His voice was short. He put his hand over the mouthpiece and said something.

Mike said, "Hi, Nick."

"How are you?"

"Good." He didn't sound good, but he also didn't sound like chatting.

"Wanted to let you know we went over to the house and opened the safe this morning. It was empty."

"What? Had it been tampered with?"

"Not that I could see."

"Interesting."

"Yeah. One thing you oughta know and tell your new boyfriend Holland--"

"Don't start with me."

"Sorry." I waited for a moment. "What I was gonna say is that there were fifty thousand-dollar bills. I had to order them special through Bank of America. That

108

was in January. I bet they have the serial numbers."

"That's all you had?"

"No. There was close to half a million, all in hundreds, except for the thousands."

"Did you get that all at once?"

"Most of it. Back in March of '51. They'd have most of the serial numbers. I gave some of that stash to you guys back in May of last year. And I replaced that in July. So they should have a record of that, too."

"How much last year?"

"Ten thousand on the nose."

"OK. I'll give Holland a call."

"Mike?"

"Yeah?"

"You wanna come over for dinner tonight? Just you, Carter, and me?"

He was quiet for a moment. "Yeah. I sure would."

"How about meet us at Grant and California? We'll go to the Far East Cafe."

"Yeah. I'd like that."

"See you at 7?"

"Thanks, Nick."

. . .

Just as I was hanging up the phone, Carter and my father were coming down the stairs.

"I don't care. Do what you want." That was my father.

"Nick?" That was Carter.

"What's going on?" I asked.

My father looked annoyed. He pointed his pipe at Carter. "HE wants to go rummaging up in the attic. You know, Nicholas, I'm giving YOU this house, not HIM."

I looked over at Carter who shrugged.

"So he wants to go up in the attic. What's wrong with

that?"

My father's dark eyes flashed with anger. "What is this? The pre-sale inspection?"

I crossed my arms. "No. Carter is probably curious. Just like me. I'd like to go up there, too."

"Fine! Go right ahead. You go right ahead." He didn't raise his voice, but he sounded angry and hurt at the same time. "Leticia and I will pack a bag and move into the Huntington Hotel. Then you two perverts can have the run of the whole goddam house." With that, he turned on his heel and walked up the stairs.

Carter and I just stared at him as he disappeared. "What happened?" I asked.

"I knocked on the door. He was all smiles until I asked about going up in the attic."

I heard a discreet cough. I turned and saw Zelda standing near the dining room. She nodded her head towards the kitchen. We followed her in there.

Mrs. Young was pealing potatoes and listening to the radio, which was turned down low.

Zelda sat down at the table and motioned us to do the same, so we did. In a low voice, she said, "All of your mother's things are in the attic."

I looked at Zelda. For once, her emotions were on display. She looked stricken.

"A lot has happened here very quickly. We're all reeling, Mr. Nick. When the dust settles, it will all be for the best, I'm sure. Miss Leticia will be much happier in a small home. Dr. Williams will be happy because she's happy." She stopped and looked down at the table, wiping away some non-existent crumbs. "But, I imagine that your father is very upset about having to go through all of the things that have been packed away. It might be better if you wait until they're gone before you look around."

She took a lace handkerchief from under her sleeve and dabbed her eyes. "I'll be happy to come back for two or three days and show Mrs. Kopek where everything is."

I smiled and said, "Thank you, Zelda."

Chapter 10

Far East Cafe
631 Grant Avenue
Sunday, June 20, 1954
Just past 7 in the evening

The Far East Cafe was a favorite spot for all of us. We were seated at a small booth in the middle of the restaurant. Mike and I had gone there a lot for dinner when we were living together before the war. And this was where I'd brought a reluctant Carter back in '47 to introduce him to Chinese food. He'd lived in San Francisco for eight years and had never had any until then.

Carter and I had walked down California Street and met Mike at the corner of Grant. The weather was warm and the sky was clear, which was nice.

Carter had, of course, ordered chop suey. Mike had ordered a crab dish, his favorite. I put in for my usual, which was pork and vegetables in a spicy sauce. My

113

dish wasn't on the menu but I had learned how to order it a long time ago.

We were also sharing dumplings and I was slurping down their spicy soup that I loved so much.

Only Mike could use chop sticks. I had tried and could never figure it out. Carter claimed his fingers were too big. But Mike could eat individual grains of rice using the long wooden sticks, which was always impressive to watch. And his fingers were just as big as Carter's.

"So, your old man blew a gasket, huh?" I could tell that Mike wasn't as won over by my father's change of heart in the last few months as Carter was. Of course, Carter hadn't been the subject of a steady stream of insults like Mike had been back in '40. I was still pretty steamed about that event and it had been fourteen years since it had happened.

I nodded. "Zelda thinks he doesn't wanna have to go through my mother's stuff."

Carter said, "She's right. I should've thought about what I was asking."

Mike shook his head. "You can't win with that man. I admire you for trying, though."

Carter stabbed a dumpling with his fork and looked at Mike. "I know you still want to protect Nick from all those years ago, but I've spent a lot of time with Dr. Williams in the last year. I wish you'd lay off him. This is a tough time. For all of us." Carter's voice was heated, which was rare.

Mike looked at me and then looked back at Carter. "Carter, man, I'm sorry. I'm still burnt about what he did back then. And, yeah, I've never given him a chance since." He deftly grabbed a dumpling and put it on the little plate in front of him. "He's your father-in-law... Or, whatever. Not mine. And, like I said, I admire you for spending time with him and all that."

I reached down and put my hand on Carter's thigh. He sighed. "Well, the important thing is to help them both get moved and then we can start building a new home for ourselves."

Mike nodded and looked off in the distance.

"So, what's happening with you?" I asked.

He shook his head. He put down his chop sticks and ran his hand over his face. "I'm beginning to think maybe I'm screwed up or something."

"Why?" I asked.

"Because I feel so paranoid about Ray. I don't know what it is. And I feel the same way about Holland." He sighed heavily as his face began to take on its monster look. "I feel like Ray is trying to make me. But I don't know why. And I can't imagine what he would gain from it."

Right then, our dishes arrived. Once we got the table organized and began to dig in on the main course, I said, "This is gonna sound a little nuts, but maybe you're not wrong."

"What do you mean?" asked Mike.

"Remember what happened at Halloween? That kid that Robert was going with was a plant by the F.B.I."

Mike shook his head. "I thought of that already. Ray's never been arrested."

Carter asked, "But he was married. Maybe he got caught in a raid and, to protect himself, he made a deal, so they never booked him."

Mike shook his head again. "No. I poked around for just that thing. If it happened, it was way off the books. Besides, those were rogue agents. It wasn't the local Bureau office. It was just a couple of guys. In the end, they were probably reprimanded for working without authority." He picked up a piece of asparagus. "Of course, the Bureau was lucky to miss the bad publicity since the S.F.P.D. got to take credit for breaking up a cocaine ring." He shook his head. "No, that's not it." He took a drink of his hot tea.

"What about Holland?" I asked.

"I don't know. It just doesn't feel right. But I can't pinpoint any one thing."

Suddenly, I remembered the conversation I'd had with the lieutenant during the fire. I told Carter and Mike what he'd said and how he'd shaken my shoulders.

"He called you by your first name?" That seemed to surprise Carter more than anything.

"Yeah. And he was personally concerned. For someone who doesn't like queers, he didn't act like it."

Mike shrugged. "Maybe he really was glad you and Carter didn't get hurt."

I shook my head. "No. It was..." I looked for the right word. "It was intimate." I looked at Mike. "It was the kind of thing you would have done. But I was in shock because of everything happening and all I could do was nod and point."

Mike looked at a crab leg and grabbed it with his chop sticks. He lifted it up in the air and examined it.

"What?" I asked.

"I was just thinking. Putting Ray to the side for a moment. Maybe Holland is really one of us."

Carter said, "That's been my assumption all along."

I turned and looked at him. "Like how you're convinced Errol Flynn is?"

Mike, whose mouth was full of crab, guffawed and dropped his chop sticks to grab his napkin.

Carter said evenly, "No, Nick. I'll admit I've got a crush on Errol Flynn. OK?" He turned towards me. "He does look like you, after all."

I'd never heard that before. I looked at Mike for confirmation. He turned his hand from side to side as if to say, "more or less." I just shook my head and turned back to Carter.

He continued, "Holland is just a little too by the book. All those firemen I worked with, Ray included... That was always one of my clues. You know the type. Always clean. Always on time. Those so-called normal guys are all slobs."

Mike said, "Hey! I'm a slob. And I ain't so-called normal. I'm a perfect Kinsey 6!"

Carter shook his head. "I've seen photos of you on your bike when you were on motorcycle patrol, Mike. That thing was spotless. And those leathers..."

I laughed. "He's got you to rights on that, Mike. That Indian was your goddam baby. And you're not a slob. You just have a lotta shit. Like books."

Mike smiled, meticulously ate three grains of rice, and said, "Fine. So, your case for Holland is that he's too perfect?"

Carter said, "Sure. He's too perfect. And now he's your best friend. You must have done something to get him to trust you."

Mike pointed at Carter with his chop stick. Someone once told me that was rude. "Yeah. I did, in fact."

"What?" I asked.

"I did what he asked me to do. I haven't bothered him about case updates. I've called him as soon as I had new information. I've answered his questions but not asked any of my own. Maybe that's all it is. Maybe he's treating me differently because he trusts me."

. . .

By the time we walked out onto Grant, the sun had set and the neon lights of the City were filling the night

117

sky. We strolled together to the corner of California. Mike said goodbye and kept going down Grant, while we climbed up California.

Once we got to Sacramento Street, we entered the house through the kitchen door. Zelda had given us both a set of keys earlier in the day.

The kitchen was empty and quiet. We passed through into the dining room and found my father sitting in front of the fire. The door to the garden was open, but the room was still warm. My father always loved a fire, even in the summer.

Without saying hello or even looking up, he said, "Have a seat, will you?" His voice was softer than usual.

I took off my coat and threw it over one end of the big sofa. As I rolled up my sleeves, Carter followed suit. We both sat down across from where he sat.

My father had placed his pipe on the little ashtray stand next to his chair. He was holding a glass of something in a crystal tumbler. I looked closer and realized it was an Old Fashioned. I got up and asked Carter, "You want something?"

Carter asked, "Is there any beer in the house?"

My father nodded and said, "Mrs. Young likes Lucky. I'm sure there's a can or two in the icebox."

I laughed. "Carter won't touch the stuff."

My father looked over at me and smiled. "You got yourself a good man there, Nicholas."

I sat back down, touched but more surprised than anything else. I nodded and said, "Yeah. I do."

My father stood up. "I wanted to see you two before any of us went to bed. I'm sorry for what I said earlier."

Carter stood up and shook my father's hand. "I wasn't thinking, Dr. Williams."

My father shook his head. "This is happening very quickly. It's a good thing. And I am glad you will be

118

here..." He smiled at me and said, "In this big pile of rocks..." I blushed. "Long after Leticia and I are gone." He looked around the big room. "It's a fine house. It'll do you proud. I promise." He drained his glass and handed it to me. "Good night, Nicholas."

I stood up and replied, "Good night, Father."

My father turned and looked up at Carter. "Good night, young man. Leticia reminded me tonight what a fine addition you are to this family of Welsh idiots."

Carter and I both chuckled. He said, "Good night, Dr. Williams."

My father looked at me for a long moment. "I love you, son."

I just nodded because I couldn't speak right then.

. . .

As we were lying in bed, Carter sighed.

"What?" I asked.

"Your father never ceases to surprise me. Just when I think he's going one way, he goes another."

"Yeah." I thought about Mike's reaction earlier and realized I was more in his camp than Carter. Of course, I liked Carter's mother much more than he did. It made sense. We each had a history with our parents that the other could never truly know about.

I whispered, "You need to write your mother."

He fidgeted and replied, "I guess so."

"And now that we have five guests rooms..." Besides the three up on the third floor, there were two on the floor below. One had been Janet's childhood bedroom and the other had been mine. "There's plenty of room for her to stay here."

"If she's invited, she'll probably stay across the street with your father and Lettie."

"She might surprise you. Like my father."

119

Carter pulled me in close. I sighed. He kissed my neck and bit down lightly on my ear. Just like I liked it.

Chapter 11

Offices of Consolidated Security
Monday, June 21, 1954
Around half past 9 in the morning

I was just about to ask Marnie to call Mike when the outer door banged open and Henry stormed in.

"Nick! That damn Rutledge is stalling again. He hasn't lifted the stop-work. I tried calling over there and his secretary won't put me through. All she'll do is take a message."

"Are the guys at the site?"

"Yes. And they're just milling around. Pam has been yelling until she's hoarse and none of them will work. They're right, of course. That would be in violation of their contract."

I nodded and grabbed my hat. "Come on. Let's go find out what's going on over there."

. . .

121

Although it was only a fifteen-minute stroll, we grabbed the first cab we found and headed down to The Shell Building. When the driver pulled over to let us out, he said, "Lotta cops here. What gives?"

I threw him a five and said, "Thanks. Keep the change." Henry and I piled out of the back and looked around. There were three patrol cars parked in front. I also recognized the car the coroner used to move bodies. I pulled Henry by the arm and said, "Come on."

The lobby was full of people milling around. I stopped at the news stand and asked, "What goes on here?"

"Big boss of Universal Construction on the seventh floor took one through the heart this morning."

"Rutledge?" I asked.

"That's him."

"They know who did it?"

"I hear it was Michael Abati. Some mob thing." He looked at me closely. "Hey! Ain't you--"

I pushed a twenty in his palm and said, "Thanks for the tip. You didn't see me, got that?"

He nodded and said, "Sure thing, Mister."

Henry and I walked back outside. There was a phone booth right at the edge of the drive that led to the building's loading dock. I pushed inside, dropped a dime, and dialed the office.

"Consolidated Security." It was Robert.

"It's Nick. I need Mike right now."

"Sorry, Nick. He went to go meet an informant."

"What about Sam? Is he around?"

"Sure. Hold on."

After about thirty seconds, I heard Sam's voice. "Hiya, Nick."

"Look. Rutledge, the President of Universal Construction, has just been murdered. You think you

122

can find out if Abati was behind it?"

"Sure." There was a long pause. "Only I don't think he was."

"Why?"

"When did it happen?"

"Sometime this morning. Why?"

"You think it was before 8:30?"

"Yeah."

"Well, then I don't think it was Abati."

I pulled the receiver from my ear and looked at it. I wanted to bang it against the glass wall of the booth. Instead, I said, "What are you not telling me, Sam?"

"Well, you know how I know Abati's muscle, right?"

"Sure."

"So, when I went over to find him and ask him about that Russell guy and whether you or that Henry was on their list and found out you wasn't--"

"What are you telling me, Sam?" This was driving me crazy.

"Well, Georgie--"

"Who's Georgie?"

"That's the muscle. He and Ike and me, you see..." Suddenly it was all clear.

"So, you're telling me that you and Ike are his alibi for last night and this morning?"

"That's right."

"I see." I was gonna have to have a conversation with Mike about all this. "So, is he the only muscle that Abati has?"

"No. But isn't Rutledge a big deal?"

"Yeah."

"Well, I don't think Abati would let anyone but Georgie do a job like that. He knows how to do it neat. Besides, if Georgie had done the other job, the body wouldn't have fallen outta the sky during the middle of the day. They'd be dredging the bay or something like that, looking for the body. Georgie ain't sloppy."

"Got it." So, in other words, if Abati had been behind Rutledge's murder, they would still be looking for the body. Or not even know there was a body to be looking for yet. I took a deep breath. "Do your thing and find out what Abati's camp knows about this. I think they were leaning on Rutledge and had scared him."

"I don't think so, Nick. But, I'll find out."

"Thanks. And, Sam?"

"Yeah?"

"Don't shit where you eat."

Sam laughed. "Yeah. You're right. But I know your taste, Nick, and I think you might understand why."

I hung up on him.

. . .

Henry and I walked up the two blocks on Market to the building site. We found a group of construction workers standing around, just inside the gate. Pam was holed up in the office and fuming.

As we walked inside, she stood up and said, "What the hell is wrong with that Rutledge guy?"

I replied grimly, "He's dead."

Her face softened a little as she said, "Oh, shit."

I nodded. "'Oh, shit,' is right." I thought for a moment. "What about the new guy?" I looked over at Henry, who was seated at his desk.

He slapped his head and said, "Of course. Troyer. I'll call him right now."

Pam sat down and asked, "Is he gonna be any better than that other idiot?"

I nodded. "I think so. From the looks of him, I'd say he was a Seabee."

Pam nodded thoughtfully.

Right then Henry said, "William Troyer, please."

There was a pause.

"This is Henry Winters. I'm over at 600 Market--" He stopped and listened. "He did? Thanks." He dropped the phone and said, "He's on his way over."

I nodded and looked around. "Any coffee around here?"

Pam said, "Of course. Folger's." She pointed to a plug-in percolator on a little table in the corner. "The rule is that if you want it, and we don't have it, then you make it."

I stood up and said, "Fair enough." As I was making a new pot, there was a knock on the door. Henry stood up and opened it.

William Troyer walked in. I looked up and was surprised to see that his eyes were red, as if he'd been crying.

He looked at me and said, "Have you heard?" He pulled out a big red handkerchief and blew his nose. Loudly.

I nodded. "Yeah. You OK?"

He waved me off and said, "Sure. That coffee?"

I nodded. "Ready in a couple. How do you like it?"

"Two sugars."

I looked at Henry who said, "Mr. Troyer, this is Pam Spaulding, the site manager."

Pam stood up and offered her hand. Troyer shook it, a little tentatively. She shook vigorously in return

"Seabee?" she asked.

He looked surprised. "Sure. All over the South Pacific. How'd you know?"

She pointed at me. "Nick. He's smart like that. He's a private dick, after all."

When Troyer looked at me, I just grinned and said, "I don't know about smart, but it's what I do."

"How'd a private dick get the cash to build his own office building?"

Pam and Henry both laughed. Pam asked, "When'd you move to San Francisco?"

I handed Troyer his cup of coffee as he blushed. "'Bout three months ago."

Pam said, "I'll explain it all to you later. You gotta a rescind on that stop-work for me?"

Troyer blew on his coffee. "No." He looked wistful and as if he was about to cry. Taking a deep breath, he said, "I needed to clear my head so I thought I'd walk down here and see what's going on. Mr. Rutledge is the only one authorized to issue a rescind. I don't know who'll be in charge now that..." His voice cracked as he pulled out his handkerchief again.

I asked, "How'd you get hired on at Universal?"

"Used to work for Mr. Rutledge back in Connecticut."

Henry said, "You don't sound like a Yankee."

Troyer gave him a half-smile. "I'm from L.A., actually. Long story. But, Mr. Rutledge asked me to come out here and work for him."

I nodded. "He was getting ready to drop Keller, right?"

Troyer nodded and looked puzzled. "How'd you know?"

I smiled. "It's what I do."

He grinned. "Yeah, right." He took a drink of his coffee. "Keller was on his way out. And I was here to replace him. Course, Mr. Rutledge said he was expanding. He was just waiting for something to happen, if you get what I mean."

I nodded. "Sure. Any idea where Keller slunk off to after he was fired?"

Troyer shook his head. "No, why?" As he said that, I could see the light bulb go off over his head. "Oh. You think maybe Keller is involved in this?"

I didn't say anything. I wanted to hear what he had to say.

Henry knew well enough to just listen. Pam was watching the whole exchange and looking entertained by it all.

Troyer's face turned from sad to angry in about three beats. "You think that S.O.B. killed Mr. Rutledge?"

I shrugged. "I dunno. What do you think?"

He banged his coffee cup down on Pam's desk. "He better hope I don't find him. Mr. Rutledge was like a father to me. I'll break the guy in half." Troyer's face was turning red.

I said, "Hold on, there. No one knows anything. I'm just trying to put some of the pieces together."

Right then, the phone rang. Henry picked it up and said, "Winters." As he waited, Troyer sat on the edge of Pam's desk. "Yes, he's here." Handing me the phone, he said, "It's Mike."

"Yeah?"

"You heard about Rutledge?"

"Yeah."

"Not alone?"

"Nope."

"Well, Sam made that call. He's adamant that Abati wasn't involved. But that was probably the last call like that he'll be able to make for a while. We don't wanna stir up a hornet's nest over there."

"Sure. What else?"

"When are you coming back over?"

"In about ten minutes, or so."

"Good. I'll tell you the rest when you get here."

I said, "Fine. Thanks." I handed the receiver back to Henry who put it on the cradle.

"Troyer, did the police question you already?"

He nodded. He was calmer but not much.

"Did you tell them about Keller?"

"No. They didn't ask."

I nodded. "If I talk to them, I'll tell them. Otherwise, you might plan on calling Lieutenant Holland and telling him sometime today."

"Who?"

"Lieutenant Holland. Isn't he the one who interviewed you?"

"No. I didn't get the guy's name. I was too broke up."

I nodded sympathetically. "Was he in uniform?"

"Yeah."

I wondered why Holland didn't interview the guy himself. I said, "Sorry about your friend. He was obviously a good guy trying to do the right thing."

With that, I put on my hat and made my way back to the office. This was Henry's job, after all. He could work out the details around the stop-work. I had my own job to do.

. . .

Mike was waiting for me in my office when I got back. I put my hat on the rack and had a seat behind my desk. "What else?" I asked.

"Gotta call from Holland right before I called you. I told him what Sam had found out."

"Good. Did he blow you a kiss over the phone?"

Mike shook his head. "Anyway, he said the slug was from a .45."

"Yeah. There's a million of those floating around."

"But this one was silver."

"A silver bullet? Who are we dealing with? The Lone Ranger--" Suddenly I stopped. "Damn." I sat back in my chair. I felt like a fool, but my eyes got wet.

"Yeah."

I shook my head. "The diaries." I leaned back in my chair and sighed.

"From your Uncle Paul?"

"Yeah. I can't believe they're gone. I shoulda put 'em in the safe here." I picked up a metal ashtray and threw it against the wall. "Damn!"

Marnie got up and stood in the doorway. "You OK, Nick?"

I shook my head. "No. But I'm gonna get OK. Thanks, doll" I tried to smile but it didn't take.

Marnie and Mike waited for me to come back to myself. When it was over, I blew my nose into my handkerchief. I tried to make it as loud as Troyer, but I don't think I did.

"So," I said as I put away my handkerchief, "The son of a bitch has my silver Peacemaker. And, somehow, he found the box of silver bullets. They were in two different places." I looked at Mike. "You know."

Mike nodded. He'd taught me to keep ammunition and guns apart from each other at home, just in case.

"I wonder what else he took, besides that and half a million dollars." I heard Marnie gasp. I ignored it because I realized what I'd just said. Sitting up in my chair, I said, "So, whoever killed Rutledge is who set the fire."

Mike nodded silently. He was obviously way ahead of me. He asked, "But, why?"

I said, "Well, if it was that sleazeball Keller, he had plenty of reasons to kill Rutledge."

"Who's Keller?" Mike asked.

I explained and he sat up in his chair. "So, you think he's the one who threatened Henry?"

I nodded. "Now we know the fire and the murder are connected."

Mike said, "It's possible that they're not."

"The gun and the bullets? The gun would have melted in that heat. Or become unusable. No. Whoever killed Rutledge broke into the house, ransacked it, and then set the fire to cover his tracks."

"What I wanna know is how anyone knew about that safe. Even I didn't know where it was."

I nodded. "Yeah. The company that built out the space for the safe wasn't the same company that installed the safe. And then we had a third guy--" I snapped my fingers. "Wait. The third guy. What was his name?"

Marnie, who had been standing there all along, said, "Hold on, Nick. I got his name here in my book."

As we waited, I looked at Mike with a smile and said, "I'm tending to agree with Carter about Holland, by the way."

Mike shrugged. "That's your opinion. Where's Carter, by the way?"

"He's at the house with his captain. His old captain, that is. And don't change the subject."

Mike shrugged again, "I don't care whether he is or isn't."

I laughed. "Oh, brother. You like him, don't you?"

Mike shook his head a little too vigorously.

I couldn't help myself. "You do! You like him."

Right then, there was knock on the door. As I hooted a bit, Marnie stood up and answered it. I stopped laughing when I saw who it was. Without anyone saying anything, Mike turned beet red. I started laughing again.

Lieutenant Holland grinned at me, took off his hat, and asked, "What's so funny?"

I tried to get it together. "Mike. He's a real card sometimes. He can make you laugh your ass off." I waved Holland in. "Have a seat, Lieutenant."

The lieutenant looked over at Mike for a beat too long before sitting down. I asked, "What brings you over here?"

"I wanted to ask you about that silver bullet we found. Seems like one of our guys in ballistics knew you had a box of them."

I nodded. "When Colt made the gun for my Uncle Paul, they included a gross of silver bullets. He didn't buy the gun to use it. And, I'm sure he knew that silver bullets are for show, as well. I figure he gave away a couple of boxes here and there so that, by the time they came to me, there was only one box left."

Holland said, "Your uncle must have been quite a character."

Mike snorted and I laughed. "You have no idea."

"So, that means the murderer is the same person who set the fire."

I nodded. "We were just talking about that. And, before I forget, let me give you another angle." I filled him in on what Troyer had said about Vernon Keller.

After I was done, the lieutenant sat back in his chair and nodded thoughtfully. "So, it could be this Keller who did everything?"

I nodded. "Marnie? What'd did you find out about the guy who built the mechanism?"

She stood up and walked into the doorway. I said, "Lieutenant Greg Holland, this is my secretary, Marnie Wilson." He turned and nodded politely.

She smiled and then looked at me. "Remember that guy? He was kinda crazy?"

I thought for a moment and then it came to me. "Sure. Thin as a rail. Had a nervous tic. Real egghead."

"That's the one. His name is, get this, Randolph Keller."

The lieutenant started in his chair. "Coincidence?"

he asked.

Marnie said, "Nope. According to Polk's, he and a Vernon Keller both live at the same address out in the avenues." She handed the lieutenant a piece of paper.

He looked impressed.

Chapter 12

564 33rd Avenue
Monday, June 21, 1954
A little before noon

The lieutenant pulled his car into a space a couple of houses north of where the Keller brothers lived. He drove a forest green '49 Chrysler Windsor coupe. He'd invited Mike and me to go with him to see what we could find out. The two of them had sat in the front while I'd slipped in behind Mike. I tried not to read too much into it, but it was interesting when Holland threw his arm across the back of the front seat. For a guy who supposedly didn't like queers, he had certainly taken a shine to Mike. They'd joked with each other the entire time it took to drive down Geary to the Outer Richmond.

We piled out of his car. Mike and I followed in Holland's wake as he walked up to the house. All the houses on this block, between Anza and Geary, were basically the same. Two stories. Garage on the ground floor. Sitting room window above that and overlooking the street. This house was painted a faded blue. Unlike most of the others, there were weeds growing between the cracks in the pavement out front.

The lieutenant walked up to the front gate and pressed the buzzer. Getting no answer, he pressed the buzzer again. I moved out towards the street and casually looked around. I was pretty sure I saw someone move behind lace curtains covering the bay of sitting room windows. Holland pressed the buzzer a third time.

There wasn't much we could do at this point, so Holland pointed to the car and we silently followed him. Once we were packed in, he said, "Let's find a phone. I got a trick up my sleeve."

Driving up to Geary, Holland turned right. Pulling in front of a fire plug at the corner of 32nd Avenue and leaving the keys in the ignition, he jumped out and walked into the phone booth on the corner.

As we waited, I said, "Parking in front of a fire plug. Carter would be throwing a fit right now if he was here."

"And, he'd be right," said Mike.

"You're not gonna stick up for your boyfriend?"

"Nick, I swear."

"Did you see how he put his arm over the back of the seat?"

"No. I was facing forward and minding my own business."

Holland opened the door, jumped back in, and asked, "Minding your own business about what?" He was grinning. Again.

Mike replied, "Nick's being annoying."

Holland looked at me over the back of the seat. "I can

see how he could get that way." He grinned at me and winked. I just shook my head. This guy was being mighty flirty. That was no lie.

"What's next?" I asked.

"We wait."

"Next to a fire plug?"

"Sure. Do it all the time."

"You better not let my husband catch you doing that." Mike shook his head when he heard me use that word.

"Husband?" asked Holland. I couldn't tell if he was offended or not.

"Well, we might as well be married. So, yeah. Husband." I wasn't gonna back down.

"Huh." It was an oddly noncommittal response.

We sat there in silence for a long, uncomfortable moment before Mike asked about the Brooklyn Dodgers. They started talking baseball. I nodded off.

I was awakened by the Lieutenant's voice. "There we go."

When I opened my eyes, he was pointing at something. I followed his finger and saw a Pacific Telephone maintenance truck pull up on 32nd Avenue. The driver parked at the curb, hopped out, and made his way over to the phone booth. Holland got out and walked over to where the other man was standing.

As they talked, Mike turned around and looked at me. He had that scary monster look on his face. "You did that on purpose."

I stretched my arms and asked, "Did what on purpose?"

"That crack about Carter being your husband."

I smiled and shook my head. "Not, really. It just popped out. But, did you hear how he replied?"

"You sound like a teenage girl, Nick." He was not

happy.

"That man is a homosexual, Mike. And he likes you." He was right. I did sound like a teenage girl.

Mike turned around in his seat and let out a big sigh. "Fine. You're right."

I reached over and patted him on the shoulder. "When he gets fired--"

"No. Not a good idea."

"What's not a good idea?" Holland was making a habit of coming in at the worst possible moments. Or best possible, depending on your perspective.

I couldn't help myself. "We were just talking about a prospective new hire."

"Yeah?"

"Yeah," I continued. "We pick up cops and firemen when they get caught in raids and the City cans them."

This made Holland visibly uncomfortable. "Sure." He cleared his throat. "So, this installer is someone who's helped me out before. Do either of you have any spare cash? I can reimburse you once I fill out an expense report."

I pulled out a hundred and passed it over the seat.

"That's a little too rich for the City, Nick."

I said, "That's the smallest I have. It's on me this time." I watched the telephone man as he dialed a number in the phone booth. "So, what's he gonna do?"

"He'll call the house and tell them he's checking on some trouble on their line."

Mike asked, "People buy that?"

"Sure. Doesn't seem to work in an apartment building, for some reason. But in a single-family house, people believe it. Particularly out here where folks are so trusting." He grinned at Mike, who reddened slightly.

"So, what does he do?" I asked.

136

"He goes in, checks things out, comes back, and reports on what he found. If he finds anything I can get a warrant on, I have a judge who'll usually play ball."

We waited for about fifteen minutes. Holland and Mike talked more baseball. I managed to stay awake this time. I wasn't interested in sports of any stripe. I was, however, interested to note that Holland seemed to know a lot about Joe DiMaggio's marriage to Marilyn Monroe and how it probably wouldn't last.

Just as he was talking about Jane Russell and the infamous gymnasium scene in *Gentlemen Prefer Blondes*, there was a knock on Mike's window. It was the phone installer. Mike rolled down the window as the guy leaned in.

"Sorry, Lieutenant. Place was neat and clean. One guy there. Didn't believe me. Very suspicious."

I asked, "What'd he look like?"

"Tall. Thin. Slimy fella. Had a thin mustache."

"Did he have a nervous tic?"

"This guy? No. He was smooth as a snake, if you know what I mean."

Holland reached over Mike and pushed the hundred in the installer's hand. "Thanks, Bill. Sure do appreciate your help."

Bill looked surprised when he saw how much it was. But, he took it in stride. "Sure thing, Lieutenant. Let me know. Any time." He saluted Holland and walked back to his truck.

. . .

Holland dropped us off on his way to the Hall of Justice to see if he could get a warrant. He said we wouldn't be involved if he got one. That was fine by me. I prefer to let the experts do their jobs.

When we walked into the office, my nose was hit by

137

the smell of smoke. Carter was standing by my desk and next to a wooden crate that had traces of soot on its side. His face had smudges on it and his hands were dark.

"What's that?" I asked.

"It's a goddam miracle, that's what it is. I found your Uncle Paul's diaries. They got trapped under the bookcase they were on. Somehow that created a pocket that even escaped getting wet. I found them on the first floor because the second floor had given way."

I looked in the box and couldn't believe what I was seeing. I pulled out the first three volumes and held them close to my chest. The leather bindings were definitely smoky. But there they were.

And then I started crying. And so did Carter. And Marnie, too.

. . .

Once we were all done with that, Carter showed me the other books he'd found. They'd all been together, which made sense, as they'd all been on the same shelf. I tended to keep my usual favorites all together. These were all books that Mike had given me, including *Leaves of Grass*, which I was happy to have.

"Did you find your dwarves and dragon book?" I asked.

Carter shook his head. "What's in that crate is all that I could salvage. Not counting the basement, of course. And some of the things in the kitchen. But no clothes. Nothing else. That's it."

He sat down in the chair and blew his nose. He said, "But did you see that little black book?"

I looked in the box. I found it under *Moby Dick*. "Look at that." It was the one I'd found after Taylor Wells had been murdered in Mexico the previous summer. "I guess I should go through this at some point."

Carter shrugged. "Why was it on that shelf?"

"Because I kept meaning to look through it. Should I toss it?"

Carter shook his head. "Keep it. You never know..."

I walked over to Marnie and said, "Can you put the diaries and that black book in the safe? I'll figure out what to do with them later."

She nodded and said, "Going home?"

"Yeah. I think we've done enough for one day, doll."

She smiled.

. . .

As we drove the short distance back to Sacramento Street, Carter asked, "Do we need to be driving back and forth like this?"

I nodded. "Yeah. When we need the car, we need it. Besides, we'll be moving down to Market Street before long."

Carter pulled the car into the driveway that led down to the garage. In the keys that Zelda had given us was one that, when inserted and turned, opened the electric door to the garage. He parked in the usual spot. I noticed that my father's car was out.

As we walked up to the stairs to the kitchen, I asked, "Do you wanna finally buy yourself a car?"

Carter, who was coming up behind me with the box of books, said, "Yes. But I want to buy two."

"Two? What do you need two for?"

As I opened the kitchen door, I was surprised to see that it was empty. It was just past 3 in the afternoon and, normally, Mrs. Young and the kitchen maid would be cooking up a storm. As we moved inside, I found an envelope on the long wood table. It was addressed to us both.

I opened it and read it out loud to Carter as he put the box on the table:

Dearest Sons,

Your father and I awoke early this morning to the realization that it is time to take our leave. We have decided to take a very slow drive down to Carmel and then onward to Big Sur and, perhaps, to Coronado Island. We will be gone for some time and don't precisely know when we shall return.

Your father released all of the staff and paid them, quite rightly, a year's severance as you had promised. Their last act was to help us move all of our belongings into the middle guest room on the second floor to be called for later.

Your father says to tell you that this 'big pile of rocks' is now yours. This will, of course, be formalized legally on our return.

Enjoy your new home. We will telegram, from time to time, so you will know that we are well.

With fondest love and affection,

Your Lettie

At the bottom, my father had scribbled his own note:

I will take care of 'the mountain' later. Please don't bring one of your friends over to safe crack it, if you don't mind.

I looked at Carter who looked at me. He knocked my hat off my head with one still slightly grimy hand and then lifted me in the air like he'd done on Saturday. Shifting me into the traditional bride carry, he walked through the dining room and into the great room, taking great loping strides, and opened the garden door. The wonderful thing about the garden was that it was completely secluded. There was no way to see into it as it backed up against a wall with no windows. We took advantage of that fact and enjoyed ourselves out in the fresh air for once.

. . .

Neither of us was comfortable using the bathroom in the master bedroom, so we went up to the third floor and got cleaned up. Once we were dressed, we walked down to the second floor. Before we could even start exploring the house, the phone rang. Since there was no Zelda to answer it, we both hopped down the long semi-circular staircase.

I picked up the phone and said, "Yeah?"

"Nick?" It was Marnie. "I was actually calling for Mother. Where's Zelda?"

I explained where everyone was. When I was done, she said, "I wondered about that. Mother didn't tell me but she was acting fishy last night. So." She paused. "How does it feel?"

I looked around and then up at Carter, who was grinning. "Empty. This is a huge house with no one in it."

"Do you want me to call Mrs. Kopek and have her come over tomorrow?"

I replied, "That would be swell, doll. I think I'm gonna cook a big dinner for my husband while I still have the chance."

Marnie giggled. "Oh, Nick."

. . .

I looked through the cupboards and the icebox. It appeared that Mrs. Young had cleaned us out. I couldn't blame her. She probably thought it would otherwise go to waste. I had no idea what she thought Carter and I would be getting up to but I'm sure it didn't include anything as mundane as eating.

Carter, who had been in the office, walked in and asked, "What's for dinner, Boss?"

"Ernie's, I think. We're plumb out of everything and I don't wanna go to the market."

Carter smiled and said, "Ernie's it is."

. . .

We ended up at the Top of the Mark. Ernie's was closed on Mondays.

As we sat in the window and gazed out over the City, I said, "Now about those two cars. What do you need two for?"

Carter, who was cutting into his large Porterhouse steak, said, "I figure I need something reliable. I'm thinking a Mercury. Or maybe a Pontiac."

"Not a Buick?"

Carter said, "We can't be an all-Buick couple."

"Why not?"

"It's un-American or something."

I laughed. "What's the other one?"

"Well, I want a car to play in. Something to drive up and down the coast. Some little European number. I'm thinking a Sunbeam."

I nodded. We'd seen one at a house party we'd been to in Mexico. They were a little small for my taste.

"You think you'll fit behind the wheel?" It was a legitimate question.

Carter shrugged. "Won't know until I try."

"Who sells them around here?"

Carter shrugged again. "I'll find out."

I smiled and looked out the window again. Somehow, I was thrilled and it wasn't the thing I was expecting. I couldn't believe that we would be going back to my home, my house, the place where everything began and that it would be our home. Never, not once, in a million years would I have imagined this would happen. And, yet, it had.

I put my hand next to my plate. It was as far as I dared reach. I wanted to lean over and pull Carter across the table. I wanted to push all the plates on the floor and have him take me right there, at the Top of the Mark, overlooking the City. I wanted to stand up

143

and offer my hand and have him sweep me off my feet to the sounds of "You're The Top," the song coming from the fingers of the pianist. I wanted to dance all night until my feet ached. I wanted to kiss my husband in front of the maitre d', our waiter, the bartenders, and George fucking Hearst, who was steadfastly not looking at me from three tables over, and make a complete fool of myself.

But, instead, I tapped my fingers on the table to the rhythm of the song and looked at my husband who was sawing into the overcooked piece of shoe leather that cost nearly five bucks. It was sheer heaven.

Chapter 13

Marnie was handing me a cup of coffee when the office door opened. Lieutenant Holland walked in and asked, "Is Mike Robertson here?"

I said, "Come in Lieutenant. Have a seat."

He nodded at me with a tight smile but didn't move. With his hat in his right hand, he instead said, "I just wanted to find Mike. Is he around?"

I looked at Marnie, who said, "He's meeting with a client down in Livermore this morning. He'll be back around 3 or so, at the latest."

Holland ran his free hand through his hair. For the first time, I noticed he was looking disheveled and rumpled. I wondered if he'd slept in his suit of clothes.

I stood up and walked towards him. He backed up a step when I did, as if he was afraid of me. "Did you get

145

that warrant yesterday?" I asked.

Holland looked confused at first. Then he nodded. "Oh, sure. When we went to serve it, he'd skipped. And we didn't find anything. No money. No gun. Not even the silver bullets."

"You think we spooked him?"

"Yeah. I suppose. Look." He took in a ragged breath. His eyes were red and bleary. "Can you have Mike call me when he gets back from Pleasanton?"

"Livermore," I corrected.

"Yeah. Sure. Just have him call me, will you?" He quickly put his hat back on and left.

I held up my hand to keep the office quiet and waited two beats. Then I quickly opened the door and walked towards the elevator where Holland was waiting.

"Lieutenant." He didn't turn.

"Greg." This got his attention.

"What is it, Williams?"

"You OK?"

He looked straight ahead at the elevator door. "Sure. I'm fine."

"You don't look fine."

The car arrived and the door opened. The lieutenant walked in without replying. As the doors closed, I said, "Take care of yourself, Greg."

He looked up at me, nodded, and was gone.

. . .

"What was that about?" asked Marnie.

"That, doll, was the look of a man in love with another man." I thought for a moment. "Maybe for the first time in his life."

"Gee. He's in love with Mike?"

I nodded.

"What about that Ray?" She looked around carefully,

146

as if Ray might be lurking nearby. He wasn't. He was out with Carter and Martinelli. They were doing one more pass over our house. Carter was using it as a training exercise for Ray.

I shrugged. "I don't know."

"You think Mike is... You know... Does he feel the same way?" For as long as we'd worked together, this was a topic that still made Marnie uncomfortable.

I nodded and leaned against the wall. "I do."

Robert, who'd been quietly sitting at his own desk throughout all of this, piped up and said, "I've seen guys go through that before. It's tough."

"What about you? Did you always know?" I asked.

Robert nodded. "Always. There was an older kid who lived next door that I really liked when I was four years old. I didn't know why, of course. What about you?"

I smiled. "Same. Only it wasn't the kid next door. It was my father's chauffeur. Back in those days, he wore--" I looked over at Marnie, who was turning pink. "Anyway, yeah. I knew when I was probably four, too."

Robert asked, "Was Carter in love with Henry when they were kids?"

I shrugged. "He's never said. But I know that Henry was in love with Carter. He's told me as much. And he still is."

Robert looked down at his desk. "Oh."

I laughed. "Not in that way, Robert. He's in love with Carter the way I love Henry. Like brothers."

Robert looked up and smiled. "Oh. Yeah." He seemed to remember something. "Can I get your keys, Nick? Marnie wants a copy of them for Mrs. Kopek."

I pulled the set for the house out of my pocket. He caught the jangling ring as I tossed them over. "Wow. That's a lot."

I nodded. I pointed out which ones I knew about and

which ones I didn't. He noted each one and, using an Indian ink pencil, made markings on each key that corresponded to his notes. I said, "Make a set for you and a set for Marnie, as well."

He stood up and said, "Will do. I'm going over to get them cut right now. Anyone need anything?"

I walked back over to my desk and said, "No," over my shoulder as he left. I sat down for a moment and then had an idea. Grabbing my hat, I said to Marnie, "I'm going out for a while."

"Where to?"

"To find a cop before he does something stupid."

. . .

McKeegan's on Commercial was known to be a hang-out for the cops from Central. It was nearby and off the beaten path. I wasn't sure it would be the spot to find Greg Holland. I wasn't sure whether he'd want to talk to me. He'd treated me like the plague at the office. But I thought I'd give it a shot.

The cab dropped me off at the corner of Commercial and Montgomery. I walked down Commercial half a block and pulled open the door. Even though it wasn't even 10 in the morning, the place had a small crowd. The jukebox was playing some western swing tune I'd never heard before.

Sure enough, right at the far end of the bar, there was Lieutenant Greg Holland. He was nursing a beer and looked pitiful.

I walked over and sat down next to him. I motioned to the bartender.

"What'll it be, Mister?"

"Burgie. In the bottle, if you got it."

"Sure thing, Mister. Comin' right up."

I nodded and watched the bartender as he reached

into a cooler and pulled out a brown bottle. He popped the cap off and brought it over. "Glass?"

I shook my head and put down a five. The bartender looked at it suspiciously and said, "Want anything else?"

I said, "Not right now. But, thanks."

He scooped up the five and said, "Let me know."

I nodded as he walked off.

Holland quietly asked, "That how you buy your friends?"

I took a sip of beer. "You know, I met Mike when I was a kid on the street."

"That so?"

"Yeah. My old man was gonna kick me out so Mike took me in. He was on beat patrol at the time."

"Beat? There's a photograph of the 1940 motorcycle patrol squadron on the wall down from my office. He's the tallest one in the group."

"When I met him, he'd gotten in trouble and--"

"Your fault?"

I laughed. "No. It was someone else but you're not far off. But, yeah, when he was back on motorcycle patrol, he always used to get a sore back from crouching on that damn Indian all day."

Holland raised his bottle up and waved it in the air. The bartender brought him a new one. It was Lucky which, like Carter, I couldn't abide the taste of. After he'd taken a swig, he said, "You never answered my question."

"Yes, I did. My best friend in the world is Mike Robertson. And he became my friend when I didn't have a pot to piss in."

"He just thought--" Holland stopped as a small crowd of cops in uniform walked by. I kept my head down as a couple of them patted him on the back.

149

Once they were gone, I said, "You're probably right. But that was fifteen years ago. The only trouble we've ever had was when I enlisted in '41."

"Why was that?"

"Because I didn't tell him. I went down on that Tuesday morning and signed up for the Navy. When he got home that night, I told him. He decked me. Hard."

Holland chuckled. "Oh, I'd have paid top dollar to see that."

I waited. He was trying really hard not to like me, for some reason. It was a full 180 from his attitude the morning before. I didn't give a damn why. But I guessed that I was too exposed for him to be close to. All the world knew who I was and what I was. And it scared him.

I couldn't blame him. Whatever the real source of his fear might be, it was tearing him up inside. That much was obvious.

I sat for a moment and considered what to say next. I was curious, that was for damn sure, but I didn't want to scare him off. So, I sat for a while longer. I didn't have anything to do. I could wait.

Finally, Holland banged his empty bottle on the bar and stood up. He threw a buck down and walked towards the door. I waited until he was out the door and then I followed him.

Once I was out on the street, I saw him walking halfway to Montgomery. When he got to the corner, he turned left instead of right, going away from The Hall of Justice and the Central District Station and heading south. I wondered where he was off to, so I followed him.

Maintaining my distance, I walked with him all the way down to the building site, which was buzzing with activity. Obviously, the stop-work order had been lifted. From a few stories up in the skeleton of the building, I could hear Pam chewing out someone.

He went up to the construction office and knocked on the door. I held back at the gate and waited. When no one answered, I walked over, up the steps past Holland, and opened the door.

"Come in, Lieutenant." I sat down on Pam's desk and waited.

He stood in the doorway. His eyes were still red. Finally, he walked in, pulled the door closed, and locked it. I wondered if he was gonna try to clean my clock or put his tongue down my throat.

He turned around and stared at me. As he did, tears ran down his cheeks. I sat perfectly still, waiting for him to decide what to do.

He stumbled forward and got up in my face. His breath was sour from no sleep and too much beer. I looked up at him as he began to weave a little.

I got off the desk and pulled a chair behind him. Shoving him it, I went over and started making coffee. As I was opening up the can of Folger's, I heard him stand up. Before I could do anything, he had put his arms around me and was burying his face in my neck.

I gingerly pulled him off me and turned to face him. The tears were still coming.

I nodded and said, "I know."

It was like watching a storm blow through. It was going to happen. It had to happen. And all anyone could do was let it happen.

After a few moments of us standing there looking at each other, he ran the sleeve of his coat over his face and sniffed. He walked over and sat down. I turned around and finished making coffee.

Once it was ready, I poured him a cup. "How do you take it?"

"Black," he croaked.

I handed him the cup and said, "Drink some right now."

He nodded and did so. It was hot, so it likely burned his mouth, but he drank it nonetheless.

I pulled over the other chair and sat down in front of him. I pulled out my pack of Camels and offered him one. He shook his head and said, "Don't smoke."

I put the pack back in my coat and said, "This your first?"

He sat back and looked at me. "My first what?"

"Your first love."

The tears started again. I took the coffee cup from his shaky hand before he spilled it. I said, "Greg, it's hard to admit the truth, isn't it?"

The lieutenant nodded. He sniffled again and looked around for a paper tissue. I handed him my handkerchief. He wiped his face with it and then did something curious. He smelled it.

Looking at me like a kid, he said, "It smells like you."

I smiled and asked, "How so?"

"It smells like cigarettes and soap. Like you smell."

"How does Mike smell?" I asked. I felt like I was probing the wound. I wanted to just lance it and not cause more harm.

He sighed. "Like leather."

I nodded. "Yeah. He still wears his motorcycle jacket, without the patches, of course. I think he keeps it in the closet with his other coats."

Holland smiled. He was attractive. But, as I'd noticed before, it was in a nondescript way. I looked at his broken nose. "You used to box?" I asked.

He put his hand on the bump on his nose and asked, "This?"

I nodded.

He shook his head. "Got in a fight when I was 18. Someone called me a..." He couldn't finish.

"A faggot?"

He nodded.

"Mike taught me how to take care of myself around people like that."

Holland laughed wryly. "Are you trying to sell me on him or something?"

I shrugged. "Maybe. I'm telling you know it's all OK."

He stood up and began to pace in the small office. "No. It'll never be OK. You have no idea."

I crossed my arms. "Try me."

He stopped and looked down at me. Taking a deep breath, he said, "I'm being blackmailed."

This, I wasn't expecting. But it made more sense than just puppy love.

I said, "Have a seat and tell me what's going on."

He stood there for a moment. Finally, he sat down, looked at the floor, and began to talk.

"It started in January. I was walking down Polk Street one night and heard someone call my name. When I turned around it was a man I'd once met. His name was Roger Steele. We'd met at a private party. I was there undercover. We got to talking at the party and he invited me to his house. I'd already been having second thoughts about the investigation. I was considering whether to hand in my badge and just walk away." He looked up at me. "I even thought about calling you to see if I could get a job. I wanted a safety net before calling it quits. Know what I mean?"

I nodded.

"So, Roger sees me on Polk Street and asks, you know, if I wanted to come see him again. I had been out walking just for the fresh air and to clear my head and didn't want company, so I declined. Somehow he'd found out I was a policeman and he told me so right there. He told me that if I didn't come with him right then, that he would call my captain." He sighed deeply and looked up at me again.

"What'd you do?"

"What could I do? I went home with him. We did what we'd done before which was easy for me." He looked at me as if he wondered if I needed it spelled out.

I didn't. So, I asked. "Then what happened?"

He quickly smiled at me. "By the way, your technique isn't bad for a private dick." He seemed to think that was funny. But I didn't smile. I just watched and waited.

He cleared his throat. "He found my phone number and started calling me at home. He wanted me to come over once a week. Then it was twice a week. The thing was, he wasn't ugly."

I shook my head. "That doesn't mean a thing. You didn't wanna do it. That's what matters."

"You make it sound like rape."

I nodded. "In a way, it is."

"But--"

"I know."

"Well, I guess it was in March that I realized I just couldn't do it anymore. I stopped answering the phone, which got me in trouble with my captain. The next thing I know he's sending me a letter." He shook his head. "It was like in the movies. Letters cut out of the newspaper. That sort of thing."

"What'd it say?"

"That I could just send him fifty dollars a week, instead."

"That's a lot."

Holland ran his hand over his head. "Yeah. It is."

"Did you pay?"

"Yes. And I'm still paying. I send it to a post office box. Every Monday."

I shook my head. "For the love of Mike, you're a cop. I can count at least three state felonies and two federal ones. Why not bust him?"

Holland's face went white. "I couldn't. He'd tell my captain. It'd get in the *Examiner*."

I nodded. "Probably so. But," I put my hand on his knee. "You do have a safety net. In the car yesterday, you were the new hire we were talking about. Or, to be honest, the one I was talking about."

Holland sat back and closed his eyes. "I don't know."

"Have you ever been married?"

He sat up and opened his eyes. "Yeah. I was. We got married before the war started."

"What happened?"

"She said that she lost faith in me. Because I didn't go off to fight." He frowned. "I did what my sergeant asked me to do and didn't enlist."

I nodded. "Same as Mike. And Carter."

He shrugged. "Maybe if I'd gone, she wouldn't have left me."

I snorted. "Is it possible she knew you weren't interested?"

He stood up and looked out the window built into the office door. He put his hands in his coat pocket. "Yeah. I hadn't thought of that. But that probably was it."

"How did it happen? Did she go to Reno?"

He turned around and smiled. "Yeah." He looked down at me. "Why are you asking me about this?"

I stood up and crossed my arms. "I want you to remember that you were in a bad situation before and got out. This'll probably be like ripping off the bandage but it'll be a hell of a lot easier. Like I said," I put my

155

hand on his arm. "You gotta safety net. Only thing is, you'll have to work for me. I know you don't like me but you can't work for Mike. You know how that is."

He grinned, reached over, and pulled me into a bear hug. He really needed a bath. After patting me on the back, he let me go. "I never said I didn't like you, Nick. I was scared shitless by you. That's all."

. . .

After checking in with Pam, who was in rare form and having a great time doing her job, I decided to go back to the office. By then it was past noon. Holland was following me around like a puppy, so I invited him to lunch at The Old Poodle Dog since it was just around the corner from the construction site.

The original Poodle Dog had been a fixture of the Gay Nineties. It was a French restaurant that also included private dining suites on the upper floors. There were plenty of references to the place in Uncle Paul's diaries. He'd seduced a number of men there. It had been originally located at Eddy and Mason. The '06 fire destroyed the building. The current spot came along in '33. I'd been there a couple of times. Although it was a nice spot, I was sure it was a shadow of its old self.

Once we were at a table and had some coffee, Holland began to pepper me with questions about Mike. He had it bad and it was sweet, I had to admit. I answered his first couple of questions, then I put out my hand.

"Hold on, cowboy. These are questions you need to ask Mike. Besides, you don't want to be grilling the ex about your new squeeze, right?"

"But you're his best friend."

I had to smile because, just like the day before, we were in school girl territory. I replied, "Yeah. And since he's my best friend, I don't wanna spoil any possible first date conversation for him. He deserves to tell you about himself while he grills you about you. Got that?"

Holland nodded and took a sip of his coffee. He looked around the restaurant and then back at me. "Possible?"

I nodded. "You bet. He's living with Ray. They're an item."

Holland's face fell so hard you could almost hear the sound of a brick hitting the pavement. "Buck up, Holland. I'm on your side. Ray is fine, as far as it goes, but--" Right then, our waitress arrived with our lunch.

After we were set up and Holland was cutting into his steak and French fried potatoes, I asked, "What are you gonna do about work and that letter?"

He swallowed his bite and said, "After I talk to Mike, I'm gonna come clean with my captain and turn in my badge and gun."

"Are you sure you have that in the right order?"

Holland looked at me. "What do you mean?"

"Shouldn't you take care of your own business first?"

"What if Mike doesn't like me?"

I shook my head. "Is that really your first priority?" I lowered my voice. "You're being blackmailed, bud. That's a big deal."

He put his fork and knife down and stared at me. "Oh my God. I sound like a little girl, don't I?"

"You sound like a man in love for the first time."

He looked at me and nodded. He glanced around the room again. A puzzled look came over his face. He quietly asked, "Do you know if Abati is tailing you, Nick?"

I shook my head.

"There are two mugs who are watching us closely."

I shrugged. "Let 'em look."

He raised his eyebrows and took a sip of his coffee.

157

I decided to bring us back to the topic at hand. I asked, "How old are you?"

"38."

"Any family?"

He shook his head. "My parents both died back in '37. Car crash. No siblings."

"And that's when you married the girl, right?"

"How'd you know?"

I shrugged. "You from here?"

"No. Modesto."

"Okies?"

"No. My father grew up there. My grandparents had a big spread outside of town. My mother was from Sacramento."

I hadn't touched my lunch. I wasn't really hungry. But I grabbed a slice of the bread and spread some butter on it. "And this is probably the first time you've really been in love, right?"

He wiped his mouth with his napkin and nodded.

"So, my advice is to take things slowly. But, always do what's right in front of you. Mike is a maybe."

He started when I said that but I kept going. "Your life is being messed with and that needs to stop. Today. When we're done here, go back to Central and file charges against this guy. Then go to the postmaster's office where that post office box is located and do the same. Then, and only then, go to your captain. That's my advice. And, no matter what anyone says or does, remember I have you covered. You're not gonna be tarred and feathered."

He looked scared. That was good. He had reason to be. But it was all gonna work out. Or that was what I hoped.

Chapter 14

Offices of Consolidated Security
Tuesday, June 22, 1954
Around 2 in the afternoon

"Where were you?" That was Carter. He and I were in the restroom on the third floor. He was cleaning up after going through the house for a third time.

"Chasing down Holland."

"Why?"

I gave him the highlights and ended by saying, "I sent him back to Central. I hope he does the right thing."

Carter was drying his hands. He bent over to see if all the smudges on his face were gone. I leaned over and kissed him on the cheek.

He smiled at me and asked, "What's that for?"

"No reason." I smiled back.

He looked at me for a long moment. "How's this going to work having people in the house all the time?"

I cocked my head. "Waddaya mean?"

He straightened up and looked down at me with a leer. "You know. I kinda want to go home right now and have my way with you."

I smiled back. "They can always quit if they don't like it."

Carter grinned. "I guess they can at that."

. . .

We were in the Emerald room and getting dressed when there was a knock on the bedroom door. Since he was mostly done, Carter walked over and opened the door a crack. "Yes?"

It was Mike. He pushed his way in and stalked over to me. "What the hell have you been up to today, Nick?"

I was buttoning my shirt and said, "What?"

"Holland just resigned. Why?"

I looked at my watch. It was just past 5. "That was fast."

He grabbed my wrist and turned it a little. Just enough to hurt but not enough to do any damage. Carter walked over and said, "Mike."

Letting go of me, Mike stepped back and crossed his arms. "Why did you convince him to do that?"

I rubbed my wrist. "Shouldn't you be asking Greg?"

"Greg?" Mike's monster face turned uglier than I'd ever seen it.

"Yeah. That's his name, isn't it?"

"Do you have a thing for him? Is that why you convinced him to quit?"

"Look, Mike. Has he told you why he had to resign?"

Mike shook his head. "He just said that he decided to after talking to you."

"And so you ran over here to yell at me without asking him why?"

Mike looked down at the floor. "Yeah. He said he would call me later."

"He was being blackmailed, Mike."

"What!?"

I nodded and explained what had been happening.

Mike took his hat off and threw it on the bed. "Damn it. Why didn't he tell me?"

"He tried to. He came looking for you this morning while you were in Livermore."

Mike narrowed his eyes. "And why did you get involved?"

"Because he looked like he hadn't slept. And he was acting strange. So, I went and found him at McKeegan's--"

"That dive? What time was this?"

"Around 10."

Mike seemed to finally get it. "Oh."

"After he left, I followed him to the building site. He came clean while we were there in the office. And I told him he had to go file charges."

Mike nodded. "Yeah. I'd have done the same thing."

"I also told him that he had a job but he'd have to work for me."

Mike nodded again. He looked sheepish. "Sorry, Nick. I don't know why I'm so touchy about this."

Carter slapped Mike on the back. "You're in love, son. Ain't it grand?"

. . .

As the three of us were walking down the stairs to the first floor, the phone started ringing. I watched as a young man with high cheekbones, chestnut hair, and light brown eyes walked out of the dining room and over to the phone alcove. He was was lean and stood about 5'9". He was wearing an oddly tailored morning suit. He picked up the receiver and, with an interesting accent, said, "Prospect Nine Zero Zero One." Each word was enunciated clearly.

We walked over to where he was standing and watched, like some sort of Greek chorus.

Mike whispered, "That's the kid who let me in the door." He looked like he was 25, at the most.

I looked up at Mike and winked, "Obviously, he needs better training."

He snorted.

After listening, the young man said, "One moment, please." He turned, saw us, and was startled. I saw him flush briefly as he looked up at Mike and Carter. That made me smile.

I said, "Is it for me?"

He nodded. "Yes, Mr. Williams. It is Miss Marnie. She wishes to speak with you."

"Thanks, kid."

I picked up the phone receiver and said, "Yeah, doll?"

"Who was that?"

I turned and watched as the young man disappeared into the dining room.

"I dunno. Our new butler, I think. Or valet. What's up?"

"Henry's looking for you. There's some trouble at the construction site."

"He say what it was?"

"No. He just wants you down there as soon as you can."

"Fine. Thanks, doll."

I put the phone back in its cradle.

. . .

The cab pulled up at the corner of Post and

Montgomery. I threw the driver a folded five as the three of us piled out. Work was over for the day, so the site was quiet. Henry was waiting for us at the gate. He looked pale and nervous.

"What's up, Henry?" I asked.

"It's some mob guy. DiLuca is his name. Wants to talk to you."

I looked around. I didn't see anyone. "Where?"

"Over at The Old Poodle Dog."

. . .

The restaurant was busy when we walked in. The early dinner crowd was out in force.

I walked up to the maitre d' and said, "My name is Mr. Williams. I believe my party is here already."

The man nodded and said, "Follow me." He moved across the room and to an opening with a red curtain that was marked "Private." He pulled back the thick fabric and ushered us in. We followed him up a flight of stairs, covered in a plush red carpet. The stairwell was dimly lit. The walls were covered in photographs of the old restaurant. I was pretty sure I saw one of Uncle Paul, but didn't have time to stop and look closely.

At the top of the stairs was a hallway that ran the length of the building. The maitre d' led us to a door at the back of the building. He knocked discreetly and then opened the door without waiting for a reply.

Seated at a large round table were four men. I immediately recognized Johnny DiLuca, who was one of Michael Abati's lieutenants. He was dressed in a dark suit with a red tie. He had small dark eyes, was clean shaven, and had almost no hair on his shiny bald head. I figured he was around 55.

Two of the men were obviously muscle. They looked uncomfortable in their suits and were standing behind the table. I could see guns under their coats. They made no attempt to hide them.

The fourth man was around 30 or so, handsome but pouty, and looked vaguely familiar. I couldn't immediately place who he was.

DiLuca and the fourth man had wine glasses in front of them. An unlabeled bottle of red was half full in the middle of table. Neither of the glasses had been touched.

The four of us walked into the room. DiLuca raised his hand in greeting. "Welcome, Mr. Williams." He then waved off the maitre d' who left, closing the door as he did.

"Please, have a seat. Mr. Jones. Mr. Robertson. And, of course, Mr. Winters."

As we sat in the four empty chairs, I said, "How do you do, Mr. DiLuca?"

He nodded at me. "So, you know who I am?"

I smiled. "Of course."

That seemed to please him. He smiled as one does to the hired help. "Good. These are my associates." He waved vaguely at the muscle. "And, this is Joseph Abati, my employer's son."

Now I could see it. The kid looked like his father. He also looked very upset about something. I nodded and said, "Good to meet you, Mr. Abati. How can we help you?"

DiLuca raised his hand. "No business yet. Some wine, perhaps?"

I shrugged.

"Rocco. Call down for more of this." He pointed to the unlabeled bottle of red. Rocco, one of the muscle, picked up a phone by the table and mumbled something into it.

DiLuca smiled at me. "So, I see the great fortune of

Mr. Paul Williams continues to expand under your competent guidance."

I quickly glanced over at Carter, who was trying very hard not to smile. I just nodded and said, "Thank you. I'm very fortunate." I was resorting to what Carter usually called my "high-hat" tone. It was how my father liked for me to talk.

DiLuca nodded. "Yes. Such a great fortune. I am still at a loss to understand how the court saw fit to hand it over to a known degenerate." He smiled in a particularly nasty way as he said that. Joseph Abati shifted uncomfortably in his seat.

I shrugged. "Like uncle, like nephew, I suppose."

DiLuca laughed at this. It wasn't a nice sound. "Yes. The stories of your uncle are legendary. I understand that you are moving into your father's house on Nob Hill. May I congratulate you?"

I shook my head. "I'm just doing what my father wants."

DiLuca nodded thoughtfully. "Your devotion is wise. Particularly in these times of such wild abandon among our youth. Filial devotion is a mark of respect. Don't you agree, Joseph?" He turned slightly in his chair and looked at the younger man.

"Of course, *Zio*."

DiLuca smiled at us. Again, like we were the help. "*Zio*. That means Uncle in our language. Of course, I am a close friend of the family, but no blood relation." He reached over and patted the kid's cheek. It was a curiously affectionate gesture that held an obvious threat in it.

Right then, there was a knock on the door. A waiter entered with a second unlabeled bottle. He placed that on the table. He departed without saying anything.

"Joseph, please pour our friends each a glass of

165

wine."

Abati stood up, picked up the new bottle, and did as he was told. I was hoping that everyone would be smart enough not to drink from a bottle that wasn't opened at the table. I knew Mike would. But I wasn't sure about Carter and Henry.

Once Abati was done and had taken his seat, DiLuca raised his glass. "To our new friends."

We raised our glasses in reply. I sniffed the wine and it passed the smell test. I took a small sip and put it down. I quickly glanced around. Mike and Carter did the same. Henry, however, took a whole mouthful. I took a deep breath and hoped for the best.

I saw that DiLuca and Abati both drank from their glasses. DiLuca looked at his glass and said, "From the vineyards of a friend in Sicily. Not far from Mount Etna. The volcanic soil adds a little spice to the grape, don't you think?" He looked at me as he said that.

"I don't know much about wine, to be honest."

He nodded and looked around the table. "Well, if you will allow, I would like to tell you why I asked to meet with you, Mr. Williams."

I nodded and waited.

"You see, when poor Johnny Russell fell off your building, I believe it may have led you to believe that my--" He coughed. "Our organization might have been involved. Of course, nothing could be further from the truth. Then I find out that, today, you are having lunch here, at my favorite restaurant, with a police lieutenant. And I begin to ask myself why."

I waited while he paused. I was gonna let him lead the way down this particular garden path.

"So, I thought that, perhaps, without bothering my employer, Mr. Michael Abati, that we could have a little talk about these things. Ours is not a large organization

166

but, then again, compared to Chicago or Los Angeles, San Francisco is not a large city. We have, as I'm sure you know, an understanding with the police. Neither of us likes anyone coming in from the outside."

Mike said, "Like Nick DeJohn." This was the Chicago mobster that Michael Abati had murdered back in '47.

DiLuca looked surprised. He glanced at Mike and then at me. He nodded in acknowledgment. "As the case may be, I asked you here to give you a friendly reminder to stay clear of the police. Let them do their work."

I smiled. "The man I had lunch with resigned from the force today."

DiLuca sat back in his chair. "I had not heard this."

"Yes. He'll now be working for me. That's what our lunch was about."

"I see. So you're adding another pervert to your organization, is that it?"

I didn't reply. I watched a grin pass over Abati's face and then disappear. He looked at me for a long moment. I kept my eyes on DiLuca.

"I find the increasing presence of perverts and queers in the City to be very disturbing." Mike stirred in his chair. I watched as Rocco put his hand on his gun.

I looked at the Abati kid. His face was flush with some emotion. It could easily have been shame or embarrassment. I wasn't sure. I looked back at DiLuca who seemed to make a mental note of my glance.

"You see, Mr. Williams, I am a friend of the Hearst family. I can certainly understand why they would be upset at being disturbed in public by the likes of you."

I knew he wasn't really trying to intimidate me. There was something else going on. "The likes of me?" I asked.

167

"Yes. The pervert." He glanced around the table and ended up with his eyes on Abati. I suddenly understood.

I said, "Well, Mr. DiLuca, as you know, this is a free country."

He nodded. "Of course. We live and let live. That's the phrase?"

None of us replied.

After a couple of beats, DiLuca stood up. "Thank you for your time, Mr. Williams. Please, stay and have dinner on me." Abati, who was still blushing, stood up along with the muscle and the four of us. I stepped back, getting as far away from DiLuca as I could. Mike and Carter did the same. Henry looked a little woozy. Carter grabbed him as DiLuca left the room in between his muscle. They left without saying anything else. The Abati kid glanced at me as he walked by. There was an obvious pain in his eyes. I simply nodded.

As soon as the door was closed, Mike ran over to the phone and picked it up. He barked into the mouthpiece, "We need a big glass of milk. Right now!"

Chapter 15

The Old Poodle Dog Restaurant
65 Post Street
Tuesday, June 22, 1954
Early evening

Whatever was in the wine didn't really harm Henry. It just made him feel pretty bad. A different waiter had brought in the glass of milk and got it there fast. I handed him a folded twenty and said we were leaving.

The milk seemed to help Henry a bit. We went down to Post Street. Mike took Henry over to Robert's in a cab while Carter and I walked home.

He asked, "Well, son, how does it feel to be leaned on?"

We were standing at the intersection of Taylor and Sutter. We'd walked up Post to Taylor and then turned north. The sidewalk had been packed so we'd walked in silence.

"DiLuca was trying to dump Abati's son on us."

Carter looked down at me. "Really?"

"Yeah. There was some posturing, sure. But why bring Abati along?"

"Showing him the ropes?"

I shook my head. "DiLuca wants to be the boss. He doesn't wanna train the son. He wants to get rid of him. Easier to convince us to take him that to rub him out. Less messy."

Carter shook his head and said, "Yeah. Poor kid."

I nodded. "DiLuca would already be the boss if the trial for DeJohn's murder had gone the way the D.A. wanted it to." The charges against Abati had been dropped and the case was still open.

We had just crossed Bush and were coming to the steep part of the hill so we stopped talking. When we got to California, we stopped and waited for the light to change. The early evening was cooling off fast and there was a thick fog rolling in.

We crossed the street and walked along the side of Huntington Park. When we got to house, we walked over to the side and up the stairs to the kitchen door. It was locked, so Carter used his key to open it.

When we walked in, we found Mrs. Kopek in the middle of a small group of people. Everyone was talking loudly in some language other than English. I couldn't tell if we'd interrupted a fight or what. Something smelled very good. I saw a number of pots on the stove.

When she saw it was us, she smiled, bowed slightly, and said, "Hello. Welcome home."

Everyone else in the room went silent and stared at us. Mrs. Kopek said something and suddenly they were all smiles.

"Hello. Who do we have here?" I asked.

"These are your new staff. All Czechoslovakian. I introduce." She clapped her hands and they all formed a line. It was like something in a movie.

Mrs. Kopek was dressed in a uniform of some sort. She was wearing a long gray skirt covered by a white apron. Her blouse was black, with puffy sleeves. Her head was covered by a white scarf.

There were five people in line. One was about Mrs. Kopek's age. The other four were all under 30.

The first person was the kid who'd answered the phone earlier. As Mrs. Kopek gestured, he stepped forward. She introduced him. "Gustav Bilek. Butler and valet. From Prague."

She put her hand on my arm. "Mr. Nick." I had no idea why I wasn't Mr. Williams, but I was so completely fascinated by this unfolding scene that all I could do was smile. She put her hand on Carter's arm. "Mr. Carter." Gustav clicked his heels and bowed. He then stepped back in line.

Mrs. Kopek beckoned to the next one in line.

"Ferdinand Zak. Gardener and chauffeur. From Prague." He had black hair, dark eyes, a long face and was wearing high-laced boots like my father's chauffeur wore in the 20s. He stood about six feet even and obviously had an athlete's body. Something about him made me wonder if he was a runner or maybe a swimmer. He was dressed in dark khaki trousers. His shirt was black and buttoned to the collar but without a tie. He smiled and bowed. He didn't click his heels, which made sense. I doubted the rubber soles of his boots would make much of a sound. He stepped back in line.

Next was the older woman.

"Tereza Strakova. Cook. Ostrava." This was the larger city that was near the small town where the Kopeks were from. She was wearing an outfit similar to Mrs. Kopek's. The only difference was that her thick gray hair was covered with a gray scarf instead of white. She smiled, curtsied, and stepped back.

"Ida Vanyova. Kitchen maid. Pilsen." She was blonde, had icy blue eyes, and seemed to be athletic under her long gray skirt and white blouse. She was just a little shorter than me and was also wearing a gray scarf. She didn't smile. But she did curtsy and then stepped back.

"Nora Vanyova. House maid. Pilsen." If these were sisters, they didn't look anything alike. Wearing the same uniform as the other women, she stood about 5'3" and was curvy, as opposed to Ida, who was all straight lines. She had dark hair in a mass of curls and dark, smiling eyes. She curtsied and stepped back.

Carter, who had been standing behind me, went up to each one, starting with the two girls, and shook their hands. He asked them to say their names and then repeated it back as closely as he could. I noticed that Gustav was blushing hard as Carter got to him. Ferdinand's face turned cloudy as he watched this. I tried not to smile when I saw that. As usual, everyone was smitten with Carter immediately. I followed behind him and repeated everyone's names as well. The smiles were genuine but not as enthusiastic. Carter had even gotten a smile from Ida, the tall one. I only rated a brief nod. I couldn't compete with the most handsome man in North America and I knew it.

"What time is dinner?" I asked.

Mrs. Kopek said something to Mrs. Strakova, the cook. She looked at me and said, very precisely, "Thirty minutes." She then said something else, which I didn't understand. I looked at Mrs. Kopek, who said, "We have noodles with a beef sauce. Nice potatoes. The little cabbages..." She looked at me.

"Brussels sprouts?"

She smiled and said to Mrs. Strakova, "Brussels

sprouts." Mrs. Strakova repeated the two words carefully. We all smiled at each other, except for Carter. He hated Brussels sprouts.

. . .

"Come see." Mrs. Kopek took us up to the second floor. She led us to my father's bedroom. Opening the door, she said, "Here. You stay. Your room."

I looked around. The furniture had been moved around. The Chesterfield now sat at the foot of the bed. The two leather chairs flanked it at either side. It didn't look right.

Mrs. Kopek opened the big wardrobe and said, "Here. Your clothes."

I looked inside and then asked, "What about Carter's?"

She smiled. "Next door. Each have dressing room. Good? Yes?"

I looked at Carter, whose face was wrinkled in either worry or distaste. I walked over to the big bed. It had been made up but everything looked wrong. The bedspread was placed in the wrong direction. I turned around and said, "Thank you Mrs. Kopek. It all looks fine." I hoped my face didn't show my disappointment.

She smiled. "I send Gustav when dinner ready. Yes?"

I smiled and nodded. "Yes. Thank you."

She bowed and then was gone.

Carter walked around the room. "She's never seen this house before. What about calling Zelda?"

I shook my head. "I don't think that's a good idea. Those two will butt heads. They're cut from the same cloth."

Carter was leaning against the mantel. As he did so, I walked over and stood up on my toes to kiss him. We stood like that for a while. When we were done, I said,

"I have an idea."

"What's that?"

I smiled up at him and said, "We need to call in the only woman for this job."

"Marnie?"

"She's too busy. This is going to be a full-time job for a couple of weeks."

Carter looked confused. "Who?"

"Aunt Velma."

. . .

While we were waiting for dinner, Carter decided he was going to move some of his clothes into the big wardrobe. While he did that, I walked down to the office.

"Hello?"

"Robert. It's Nick. How's Henry?"

"I put him to bed. What happened?"

I gave him the highlights. "He should be fine in the morning."

Robert said, "I hope so."

"Where are the planes?"

"The *Lumberjack* is here. The DC-7 is out."

"Great. Here's what I need..."

. . .

"Hello?"

"Aunt Velma. It's Nick."

"Well, isn't this a treat! Leroy! It's Nick."

It sounded like they were in the rumpus room. I could hear the television in the background. "Tell him hello and then go into the bedroom. I'm watchin' my boxin'!"

I smiled to myself.

Once she was situated, Aunt Velma asked, "How are

174

you and Carter?"

"We're fine. But a lot has happened in the last few days."

"Really?"

I filled her in. Once she had clucked in sympathy a few times, she said, "I'm so glad you called to tell us. I hate finding things out through the papers. They're always wrong. And so nasty."

I said, "I stopped reading the papers so I don't know if this even made it. But, the other reason I called was to ask a favor."

"Anything, Nick. You know that."

"Can you come help us out? We need to spruce this place up. I already have an interior decorator but I don't wanna turn him loose without adult supervision."

She laughed and said, "Well, I'd be happy to."

"And can you bring Carter's mother with you?"

There was a pause. "We'll see about that. But I can try."

"And a box of red-plum jam?"

She laughed. "You don't fool me. That's what you really want. But, Nick. I don't know if I can bring something like on an airplane."

"You can if I own the plane."

. . .

Dinner was fantastic. It was the best food I'd ever eaten that I could remember. Carter even tried a Brussels sprout and then had a second one. And a third. I called that progress.

The only issue we had was that Mrs. Kopek seated us at the far ends of the formal dining room table. Before the soup was served, I moved my setting next to Carter.

As we were eating our desert, which was a fluffy custard with some sort of spice I didn't recognize,

Carter asked, "Do you mind if I sit at the head of the table?"

"No. As long as we sit together."

He took a sip of coffee. "What we need is a table just for us."

I nodded and looked around. "Maybe we can have a carpenter come in and cut this table into sections. Then, when we have guests, we can expand it to fit. You know. With leaves."

He ran his big hand along the table. "Seems like a shame to cut this up. Looks like it's one piece of wood. Where did it come from?"

"My grandfather had it made for this room. It's redwood."

"Why isn't it red?"

I laughed. "It was stained dark. I don't know why. You can ask Parnell when he gets back to town."

Carter laughed at my use of my father's first name. "How do you think that's going?"

"I hope they're having the time of their lives."

Carter smiled at me and put his hand on mine. "Me, too."

Right then, Ida came out from the kitchen to collect our plates. "Good?" she asked.

Carter said, "Very good." She smiled in return.

I said, "Can you ask Mrs. Kopek to come out here?"

She smiled at me and nodded. "Yes. I ask."

As she left with the dishes, I said, "I want the story on this crowd."

Carter looked at me. "Why?"

I shrugged. "I have a feeling it's gonna be very interesting."

Mrs. Kopek came out at that moment. She walked over to our end of the dining table and looked at me. "Yes?"

I stood up. "Are you busy?"

She shook her head.

Carter asked, "Has everyone eaten?"

She nodded. "Oh, yes."

I said, "It was all very delicious." Carter nodded in agreement.

She smiled. "Very nice."

I said, "Let's go into the other room and talk for a moment."

Carter stood up and led the way. As Mrs. Kopek followed, she asked, "Is there problem?"

I said, "No. I just have some questions for you."

"Yes?"

I pointed to one of the end of the big sofa and said, "Have a seat, Mrs. Kopek."

She looked a little uncomfortable but sat down right on the edge.

I sat on the sofa a couple of feet away and Carter sat in my father's favorite chair. I smiled and said, "Mrs. Kopek, can you tell us about each of the people you've hired?"

She smiled and nodded. "Oh, yes. Mrs. Strakova is a friend from old country."

"How long has she been here?"

"Three months. She owned restaurant. Very famous in Ostrava. Government takes restaurant and she manages. Last year, she go to Italy to visit her sick cousin. Never go back."

I nodded. "And Ida and Nora? Are they sisters?"

Mrs. Kopek looked down. "No. They come in December."

"So, they're not sisters?"

She shook her head.

Carter asked, "Special friends?" This was the word Mrs. Kopek had used to talk about her son's boyfriends.

She nodded.

"The same with Gustav and Ferdinand?"

She nodded again but didn't look up.

I said, "Wonderful."

She looked up. "You like?"

I wasn't sure exactly what she meant. "I like that you've brought them all here. Did they escape?"

She nodded. "Yes. The boys and girls they have nowhere to go. Ferdinand and Ida, they were in Olympic team. Helsinki. He run. She throw--" She made a motion of someone throwing something over their shoulder.

"Javelin?" I asked.

"Yes, this."

I nodded.

"The Party find out they have special friends. They meet in special hospital for treatments." She pointed to her head. "Party want them marry, so they do. That how they leave hospital. They all escape to Austria."

Carter asked, "How did they get to America?"

"This I do not know. They arrive in San Francisco in October."

I sat back for a moment. "How long have you been doing this?"

"What this?"

"Helping Czechoslovakian refugees."

She smiled. "Oh! Since 1939 when Hitler take Czechoslovakia."

I nodded. "Well, you're doing good work."

She beamed. "You like these peoples?"

I looked at Carter who nodded. He said, "Yes. Where are they sleeping?"

Mrs. Kopek said, "In staff rooms. Downstairs."

Carter looked at me. I explained, "There are four rooms down there. But there's only one bathroom.

Right?" I hadn't been down there in a long time.

"Two bathrooms. One for boys. One for girls."

I smiled. "Good." We all sat there in silence for a moment. I took a deep breath. "Mrs. Kopek?"

"Yes?"

"Please don't move the furniture again."

She smiled. "I think I help but maybe not."

I smiled in return. "We're going to have some visitors soon. Carter has an aunt in Georgia."

She laughed. "Not Soviet Georgia." We laughed with her. This was a joke from when we first met.

"No. From American Georgia. She will be coming to visit in a few days. And so will Carter's mother. They'll be here for a couple of weeks."

"Yes?"

"Yes. Can you make sure the Rose room and the Sapphire room are ready for them?"

She looked confused.

Carter said, "Pink and blue."

She smiled at him and said, "Oh, yes."

I stood up and said, "Thank you, Mrs. Kopek."

She stood up and bowed. "Thank you. Goodnight."

We both said, "Goodnight."

I waited until she was gone before I turned to face Carter. He was standing and trying to look menacing. "My mother?"

"Payback is a bitch, you sneaky bastard."

Chapter 16

1198 Sacramento Street
Tuesday, June 22, 1954
Late evening

Carter was in the bathroom brushing his teeth while I sat on the edge of the bed. We had moved the furniture back to where it belonged and, since the evening was chilly, Carter had lit a fire. It looked like we would be keeping up my father's tradition of opening the windows and lighting fires in the summer. I liked that. So did Carter.

I sat in the darkness watching the logs crackle and pop. With the windows open, the sounds of the City were finding their way up from the street. I heard Carter drop his toothbrush in his glass and then click off the light. He sat down next to me on the bed. Putting his arm around my shoulders, he leaned in and we sat in the light of the fire for a while.

"What are you thinking about?" he asked.

"The old house. Your dwarves and dragon book. The *South Pacific* album. Mack's letters from Korea."

He ran his hand over my head and pulled me in closely. "When I was brushing my teeth, I was thinking about our first party and how Henry was moping in the kitchen and you started dancing with him. Do you know why I broke in?"

I laughed softly. "No. Why?"

"Because what I really wanted to do was to take you both upstairs and throw you in the bed."

I laughed loudly. "On that particular night, I'd have been game and I can damn sure guarantee Henry would have as well."

I sat there, next to my husband, on my parents' bed. It was actually my grandfather's. He'd had it built specifically for that room. I said, "I wonder how my father and mother felt the first night they slept in this bed?"

Carter laughed. "That's not something I wanna dwell on." He reached down and tickled me.

I laughed and squirmed for a moment. After I caught my breath, I said, "I'm sitting here because I'm afraid to get up in there."

Carter stood up. I looked at his big frame with the fire behind him. He reached out his hand and said, "Dance with me, Nick."

I stood up and embraced him. He was humming a song from *South Pacific* as we moved across the floor of the room, just in our BVDs. It was the song that offered the only possible explanation for our love. And, it was an enchanted evening, indeed.

. . .

I woke up to an insistent knock on the bedroom door. I was on my side, with Carter holding me from behind.

182

He mumbled something I didn't understand. The knock was repeated along with someone saying, "Mr. Nick!"

I realized who it was, so I said, "Come in, Gustav."

The door opened and, in the dim light of the dying embers of the fireplace, I saw that he was in an electric blue silk robe. It was tied around his body neatly and, from what I could tell, it was the only thing he had on.

"What is it?"

"It's the telephone. They ask for you."

Carter asked, "Who?"

"The police."

I said, "Go down and tell them I'll be right there. OK?"

"Yes, OK. I tell them."

He ran down the hallway and I could hear him bounding down the stairs. As I stood up and pulled on my trousers and shirt, I could faintly hear him saying, "Mr. Williams is coming soon. Please wait."

By the time I got down to the phone, I saw that Ferdinand was also up. He was dressed in just a pair of drawstring pants and nothing else. He was eyeing me as if he was afraid I would take Gustav from him. The two of them were certainly cute but neither pressed any of my buttons.

I picked up the phone and said, "Yeah?"

"Mr. Williams?"

"Yeah?"

"This is Sergeant Bullston over at Mission District Station. We have a man here who claims he set the fire at your house."

I thought for just a moment. "Is it Lysander Blythe?"

"Yeah. How'd you know?"

"Did he walk in and admit it?"

"Yeah. Can you come down--"

"Sergeant. You can save yourself a whole hell of a lot

183

of trouble by calling Central. They're handling this investigation. Blythe didn't do it. They'll be able to confirm that."

"Why would the Central guys be in on this? Ain't their district."

"The fire may be connected to the Johnny Russell murder at 600 Market Street. That was the guy who was pushed off the twentieth floor."

"That so?"

"Yeah. I'm the owner of the building. The case was being worked by Lieutenant Greg Holland." I left out the fact that Holland was no longer a cop. None of my business. Not really.

"I see."

I wondered why the hell he was calling in the middle of the night. I figured Blythe must have been making a fuss. "So, call over there. Meanwhile, my guess is that Blythe is drunk. Or maybe he's just nuts. But he didn't do it."

"Huh." The sergeant didn't sound convinced.

"By the way, how'd you know to call this number?"

"Phone company. I figured they would have a new listing for you since, you know, the fire."

"Right." I wondered who did that and realized it had to be Marnie. She really was the best.

"I'll call over to Central and see what they say."

"Let me know if I can help. But, preferably, in the morning." I put the phone back in the cradle.

I looked up and realized that Ferdinand and Gustav were still standing there, just watching me. I took a deep breath, walked over to my father's favorite chair, and turned on the floor lamp next to it. I pointed to the sofa and said, "Have a seat, boys."

They walked over as Ferdinand puffed up his bare chest and said, "We are not boys, Mr. Nick."

I nodded and sat down. "Yeah. It's just a phrase. Doesn't mean anything."

They both sat down.

"So, when did you two meet?"

Gustav said, "In the gymnasium. That is our name for the high school. I was studying for the medical school in Prague. Ferdinand was studying for the economics." He looked over at Ferdinand with adoring eyes. It was true love. On his part, at least.

"Did you go to college?" I asked.

Ferdinand haughtily replied, "Yes. The Party decided we should both become engineers so we were matriculated to the Prague Technical University."

"Mrs. Kopek said you went to the Helsinki Olympics."

Ferdinand sat up proudly. "Yes. I win the Silver Medal for marathon."

I smiled and said, "Congratulations." Gustav was beaming with pride. He tentatively put his hand on Ferdinand's knee.

I didn't think they would want to talk about being in what Mrs. Kopek had called a "special hospital," which was obviously something psychiatric. I knew that's how the Soviets were treating homosexuals. Just like was happening in America, even in San Francisco. So modern and so cruel. I was sure Czechoslovakia wouldn't want to be behind the times. So, the doctors were probably applying electric shock therapy and other horrors to people who weren't actually sick.

Instead, I asked, "How do you like San Francisco?"

Gustav smiled. "I love here. So beautiful. And so much freedom. Thank you for this job, Mr. Nick."

I nodded and smiled. "You're welcome. We're both glad you're here." I turned to his boyfriend, who wasn't smiling.

He looked at me down his perfectly-shaped nose. "So,

185

you both share the bed of your father?"

Gustav put his hand on Ferdinand's arm and said something in Czech. This gesture was ignored. Ferdinand just stared at me.

"Yeah. Tonight was the first night, to be honest."

"How are you so rich?" His tone was smug.

"I inherited it from an uncle."

"So now you take over your father's house and sleep in his bed." I wasn't sure what the kid's problem was but it was beginning to bother me.

"Sure. Why not?" Two could play this game.

"Such bourgeoisie." His voice was dripping with contempt. Gustav began to speak rapidly in Czech. His boyfriend ignored it all and kept his eyes locked on mine.

I stood up and motioned with my hand. "Stand up, kid."

Ferdinand did so and moved in close as if to intimidate me with his height. "I am not a kid, Mr. Nick."

I smiled up at him as I quickly pulled back and gave him a right hook to his left kidney that he wasn't expecting. He fell back on the couch with an expression of shock on his face. Gustav looked at me and then looked at his boyfriend. He got up, stood over Ferdinand, and spoke rapidly, obviously scolding him.

I tapped Gustav on the shoulder. He stopped and turned. I said, "Go get a towel and some ice from the icebox." He nodded and ran through the dining room and into the kitchen.

I sat down next to Ferdinand on the sofa. As I did so, his eyes began to fill up. I opened up my arms and he leaned against me and began to sob.

He had a kind of shell shock. I'd seen it before. In my own way, I'd had it. The first time Carter told me he loved me, I'd lost it. I gave him my right hook, right on the sidewalk in Sausalito, and then ran off.

When Gustav came back, he stood and looked at us for a moment. I smiled and gestured for him to sit down on the other side of his boyfriend. Ferdinand pulled Gustav into his arms and cried even harder. As the night slowly passed, I eventually fell asleep even though I tried not to.

It was light outside when I woke up. I was alone on the sofa and under a blanket. I looked over and saw Carter sitting in my father's favorite chair. He smiled as I stretched.

"Sorry, Chief. I should've come back to bed."

"What happened?"

I told him about the call from Mission Station and then about the conversation I'd had with the boys.

His face creased with worry. "Is he gonna be OK?"

I smiled. "You know better than me. You could pull him aside and tell him how yellow and purple the bruise will get."

Carter stood. He motioned for me to sit up. I did. He sat behind me and pulled me into his arms. We both lay there as the outside light got brighter. After falling asleep again, I woke up to the sounds of Carter lightly snoring behind me and someone cooking in the kitchen. But it was the smell of coffee in the percolator that got me up off the couch.

Chapter 17

Offices of Consolidated Security
Wednesday, June 23, 1954
Around 10 in the morning

"Could you add one more thing to your list, doll?"

"What's that, Nick?"

"Call Pacific Telephone and have them install extensions in our bedroom, in the kitchen, and in the office. Then have them take out the original phone. It's 1954, after all. The telephone doesn't have to be in the middle of the house."

"Will do, Nick."

"Oh, and could you see if you can find someone in London who will send us a copy of that dwarves book. What's it called?"

Robert piped up, "The Hobbit."

"That's it."

"There's a new one coming, Nick."

"Right." I'd seen something about it in the paper.

"Find out about that, too, will you, doll?"

"You want me to just call some Joe in London?" She stood up and looked at me through the doorway.

"Or Robert could," I suggested.

From his desk he replied, "I'd be happy to, Marnie."

I smiled at her and said, "Delegate. That's what Carter is always telling me."

She smiled back and said, "Yeah," as she returned to her desk.

I'd been bringing Marnie up to speed on all the changes at home. As I'd been talking, I realized how quickly everything had changed in just two days. And yet, it seemed like we'd always lived on Sacramento Street.

"Robert?"

"Yeah, Nick?" He walked over to the door.

"When does the plane leave for Georgia?"

"They left at 4 this morning. They're going to stop in Houston to re-fuel. They should be in Albany by about 5 local time."

"Marnie, can you call Aunt Velma and tell her they can leave in the morning if they're ready?"

"Sure thing, Nick."

"Thanks, you two. You're the best."

. . .

Mike walked in the office around noon. Marnie was having lunch with her boyfriend while Robert ate a sandwich at his desk in between phone calls.

I looked up and asked, "What's the latest?"

He smiled tightly and asked, "Where's Carter?"

"Down in San Mateo with Martinelli and Ray. They're looking at a warehouse fire."

He nodded. "Let's go for a walk."

"Sounds serious."

"It is."

. . .

"You get a call from Mission last night about that neighbor of yours?"

"Sure. I told the sergeant to call Central. Why?"

"Lysander Blythe is dead. His wife found him on the front porch of their house this morning. He'd been strangled."

I nodded. We were walking down Bush towards Grant and Chinatown.

"Who did it?"

"Well, here's the thing. Central is in an uproar. When Greg left, he just put his badge and gun on his captain's desk and then he walked out. Didn't even clean out his desk. Now that Mission is involved, the police chief may be called in. It's a big mess."

"How do you know about this?"

"Gotta call from Rostenkowski." He was a lieutenant at the North Station. We'd helped him out on some cases in the past.

"How's he involved?"

"He's not. But he gotta call from a Lieutenant Thomas over at Mission who knew that he was familiar with us. Thomas figured he could get some of the details that way."

"What'd you tell Rostenkowski?"

"Everything I knew."

By this time we were walking in the door at the Far East Cafe. We got seated with a pot of tea and put in our orders. All I wanted was a big plate of dumplings and their spicy soup. Mike was having the crab, again.

"How's Greg doing?"

Mike put down his teacup and frowned. "I don't know. I can't find him."

"What about Ray?"

"I kicked him out."

"When?"

"Last night when I got home."

"Where'd he go?"

"Y.M.C.A. on Turk."

I took a long sip of my tea and looked at Mike. "This thing really has me off my stride. I can barely keep up with what's going on."

"It's called shock, Nick."

I looked away and said, "I know." I told him about my encounter with Gustav and Ferdinand.

Mike laughed. "I guess I'm the only one who's never gotten that right hook."

"Of course, not. I'm not crazy."

The waitress brought our plates right at that moment. Once we were settled in, I said, "Let's go over everything."

Mike nodded as he pulled the meat out of a long crab leg. "You start."

"Last Wednesday, at 10:15 in the morning, one Johnny Russell is strangled by someone on the twentieth floor of 600 Market Street and then pushed off, landing in the middle of the construction site." I paused and thought for a moment. "Doesn't that seem sloppy to you?"

He nodded.

"Russell was on the site because he was supposed to meet Henry around 10:30 for a payoff of five grand. Henry is throwing in a grand and Universal supplied the other four. Only they sent him newsprint instead of cash dollars. Lieutenant Greg Holland from Central is on the spot rather quickly."

Mike looks at me. "What do you mean?"

"Guy hits the ground at 10:15. We're across the street

at The Palace. Pam must've called over with a message after she called the cops."

"She did. I asked her."

I nodded. "Fine. So, we get the page around 10:20 or so. Maybe later. By the time we get over there it's probably 10:30. Cops are already there and Holland is already asking questions. Doesn't that seem damn fast to you?"

Mike nodded. "Greg told me he was about two blocks away, leaving another murder scene, when the call came in over the radio."

I nodded, took out my pack of Camels, offered one, which was declined, and lit up. As I exhaled, I said, "Makes sense."

Mike took out his notebook and started making notes.

"Then Henry and I go meet with Thomas Rutledge at Universal to let him know what's happened and to take his temperature. Rutledge is the clean-cut Connecticut face of the new Universal which used to be a mob front but is now going straight. He doesn't know about the shakedown but then pretends he did all along by giving us a song and dance about hidden costs. We then meet Vernon Keller, a sleazeball who already knows about the murder and claims the man was unknown. Except, of course, Russell was the concrete supplier for Riatti Supply, which is one of Abati's companies. Keller pretends to be confused about the payoff and his boss says that it was supposed to be three grand. Obviously Keller was skimming from Universal."

Mike looked at me. "I like Keller for all of this. But not everything adds up."

I smiled and said, "Let's get the car outta the garage first. Then we can kick the tires."

Mike nodded and smiled back. "Go on."

"Next thing that happens is that, around 9 that night, Henry gets a threatening call warning him and me not to investigate."

"Who would've known you were involved?"

Using my fingers, I count out the names, "Rutledge. Keller. Holland."

Right then the waitress came to collect our plates. She sweetly asked, "More tea?"

We both nodded as she took the teapot with her.

Mike asked, "Why include Greg?"

"Where is he?" I asked, making a show of looking around.

"Dunno. Do you suspect him?"

I shrugged. "Let's keep our options open."

"Fair enough. What happened next?"

"You, being the good cop you are, get Henry and me outta harm's way. He goes to Robert's apartment. I go to the Mark Hopkins. I make two calls. One to Marnie and one to Carter down in Santa Paula. Someone listens in on my call to Carter and, truth be told, I'm sure it was the gal down in Santa Paula at the motel switchboard."

Mike grunted in agreement. The waitress arrived with a fresh pot of tea. After she walked away, I continued, "It's now early Thursday morning. I hear a noise outside the door of the suite and it's two guys who mention the name Parnell, the one I was registered under, and they know it's my father's name. They break in, I gently pistol whip them both--"

Mike interrupted with a big grin. "And tie 'em up and stuff 'em like suckling pigs."

I laughed. "You sound like a proud papa."

Mike nodded. "I taught you well."

"That you did. I knew everything there was to know about ropes before I even went into the Navy."

"And you'd only ever been on a ferry. Wasn't that nifty?"

We both laughed at that. I could feel the warm affection I had for Mike rise up right then. I poured him a new cup of tea. And then did the same for myself. "So, I call hotel security. They call Holland. I call you. You both arrive separately. Holland takes a look around and then tells you he's in love with you."

Mike, who was blowing on the tea in his cup to cool it off, looked up. "What?"

Trying to mimic Holland's voice, I said, "'I ain't one of your buddies.' He could've then easily added, 'But I'd like to be on some cold wintry night.'" I grinned at Mike who was looking at his notebook and trying to ignore me.

"Can we get back to the topic at hand, please?"

"We stop by the front desk on the way out and are informed that the manager is not available to talk with us. Even though I just got assaulted in their fine hotel. Don't you think that's suspicious?"

Mike nodded. "Yep."

"Next thing is we get word of a stop-work order from Universal. You, me, and Henry go over and find that Keller has been canned and replaced by the very dependable, and former Seabee, William Troyer who, we later discover, is an up-and-coming fellow brought in from back east to help Rutledge push Vernon out."

"You forgot to mention he hated your guts because you were a queer."

"Until I favored labor over management."

"Exactly. What's next?"

"Well this is where things get fuzzy for me, so you may have to help me out."

Mike nodded.

I continued, "Thursday evening at the office, you

195

give me a real talking to about not being a goddam baby. And then Carter gets home." I took a deep breath, remembering that evening. "We smuggle ourselves into the big pile of rocks on Sacramento. Parnell manages to maintain his cool, which still impresses the hell outta me. And Carter finally hears all about my sordid past with a 'gigantic cop' as Mrs. Young put it."

Mike shrugged and rolled his eyes. "Not everything, I'd guess."

I shrugged but smiled.

"I'll pick it up from here."

I nodded.

"Early Friday morning, you call the service and find out that your house in on fire. You, Carter, and I leave without telling anyone and find a three-alarm fire in progress. I go to Evelyn's house and call Greg."

"Who comes running because it's you and who wouldn't?" I just couldn't help it.

"Who is doing his job, Nick."

"But I'm sure the thought of seeing you made it easier to get out of bed."

Mike stopped and looked a little distressed. "He wasn't at home. I called the desk sergeant at Central who said that Greg was out in his car and that he would have the dispatcher put in a call."

I nodded. I didn't like the sound of that. I liked Greg. I liked the idea of Greg and Mike together.

Mike took a deep breath and continued, "It's obviously arson because we could all smell the gasoline and Carter later confirmed that it was."

"When Holland arrived, he was friendly to me and oddly concerned for our safety."

Mike nodded and looked over my shoulder and out the window of the restaurant.

I said, "But that could've been the crack in his shell

196

and not relief. Remember, there's more to this story."

Mike sighed. "I know." He looked at me seriously. "You like Greg, don't you?"

"I like him for you. And, he's a good cop. I'm glad he'll be working for us but it really is the City's loss."

"He's a lot different than you."

I smiled. "Or Bud. Or Ray. Or every other guy you've gone with. How're you gonna work that out?"

With a little heat, Mike said, "We haven't even been on a date yet, Nick. You practically have us shacked up and living together."

I nodded. "You're right. I do. And, having heard his blackmail story, I think you two have a compatibility problem."

He was getting angry. His monster face was emerging. He hissed at me in a low, but menacing, tone, "I'm fucking aware of that, thank you very much, Nick Williams. Now, can we address the matter at hand?"

I sat back in my chair and looked at him. "You really have it bad, don't you?"

"Yes. But it's none of your goddam business, so shut the fuck up about it."

I stood up. "I'm goin' to the can. Be right back."

. . .

When I got back, I sat down and said, "You know how much I love you, Mike. I'm sorry for sticking my nose in. I want you to be happy."

He nodded and then smiled wanly. "That's OK, Nick. I know you do. Let me do me and you do you and we'll be just fine."

"I'd kiss you right now, you big lug, if we weren't in Chinatown in the bright light of day."

He smiled and said, "OK. The next thing that happened was that Carter and his old captain

197

confirmed it was arson once the house was cool enough to walk through. We're now up to Friday afternoon."

I just shook my head. "Damn."

"I know. Greg and his cops do a canvass and all they come up with is that Lysander Blythe, your neighbor to the south, heard breaking glass at 1:30 that morning. He's also one of the neighbors who called in the fire. Around 2. Once Greg tells me this, I go over and talk to Blythe myself."

"Have you ever told Greg that?"

Mike shook his head. I rolled my eyes. He continued, "About that same time, Sam reports in and lets me know that there's no mob connection to the fire."

"Go on."

"You guys go to Union Square, by yourselves." He said that last with a tone of warning. "And blithely report that you were keeping a watch out and that you weren't followed. That still gets me."

I just shrugged.

He said, "But that does seem to confirm that the mob isn't involved."

"See?"

"No, but I'm not going to argue with you about it. Next time, if there is a next time, get backup. Got it?"

"Sure." I crossed my arms. "What happened next?"

"That night, on Saturday, we have the party at your father's house and you announce you're moving in there."

"Why include that in the story?"

"I don't know for sure, but it seems like it's part of what's going on. But I can't put my finger on it."

"The next thing that happened is very clear. We went over on Sunday morning and opened the safe. It was empty."

Mike nodded as he sipped from his tea cup. "What's

next?"

"We had dinner here and you told us about how you were feeling about Ray."

Mike shrugged, "So?"

"What if I was right? What if Ray is involved in all of this somehow?"

Mike sighed but he made a note. "Go on."

"That's when I first mentioned how Greg had been concerned for me."

Mike nodded. "Right."

"Next thing is that Rutledge is murdered. Sam and Ike, it turns out, had a date with the only mob muscle who would've been used if it had been a hit. The police confirm that a silver bullet was used. That makes it look like whoever killed Rutledge also torched the house. He ransacked the place first, found Uncle Paul's silver Peacemaker and the silver bullets. This was likely the same person who opened the safe that only one other person in the world knew about--"

"Whoa, Nick. Too many assumptions. Let's back up. What do we actually know?"

I got his point. "First, the safe was opened by someone. Only person who knew about it was Randolph Keller, brother of Vernon Keller, who live in the same house. Second, the bullet in Rutledge was silver. Third, the Keller brothers had skipped by the time Greg got a warrant to serve on them."

"Let's leave that there and move on."

I said, "Next thing is that Greg comes in the office on Tuesday morning and is a mess. He admits he loves you and is being blackmailed."

"Nick--"

"But, this is relevant. If we're gonna keep all the options open, this is a strike against him."

Mike wasn't happy but he nodded and made a note.

"What else?"

"Greg and I have a bite at the Old Poodle Dog where we're spotted by some of Abati's men. Later in the day, Greg resigns. We're summoned to the Old Poodle Dog to meet with Johnny DiLuca and Abati's kid."

"Yeah. Let's talk about that. What the hell?"

"Two things. DiLuca was sniffing around to find out what we knew about the police. I think he left convinced they knew nothing, which would be right since I don't think the mob is involved with any of this." I took a sip of my tea. It was cold.

"What's the other thing?"

"DiLuca is trying to dump Junior Abati on us. He's obviously one of us, after all."

Mike nodded. "That's my thought, too. Why bring the kid along? I'm sure DiLuca was involved in the Nick DeJohn murder and he somehow skated without an indictment."

"Did you work on that case?"

"No. It was before my promotion."

I nodded. "I don't think we were being leaned on."

"What about the wine trick?" He shook his head. "Poor Henry."

"I know. More sniffing around. Or maybe Junior did it. Who knows."

"Would you hire Abati's son? His name is Joseph, by the way. The real junior died when he was less than a year old."

"Didn't know that." I paused and thought. "No, in answer to your question, I wouldn't. That might be DiLuca's plan but I wonder what Papa Abati thinks. I doubt his dream is for his son to come work with a buncha queers."

Mike nodded. "OK. Last thing. Lysander Blythe. Why did he try to cop to setting the fire and who killed him?"

"Someone leaned on him to take the fall and, when that didn't work, they did him in." I stood up and stretched. Seemed like we'd been there all day. I put down a ten and said, "But it's kinda like pushing Russell's body off a building into a crowded construction site. It's messy and sloppy and unnecessary."

Mike nodded slowly and thoughtfully as he stood up. "Yeah. It is"

Chapter 18

Offices of Consolidated Security
Wednesday, June 23, 1954
About 6 in the evening

"You're gonna get us in so much trouble with Mrs. Kopek."

Everyone was gone for the day. Carter had locked the door and made a mess on the floor of my office when he'd pushed everything off the desk and started taking off his coat and tie. It had been a hell of a lot of fun, though.

We were dressed and picking things up. He was smiling at me in a way that made me want to repeat the whole thing over again.

"Speaking of that, Nick. Do we really need a chauffeur?"

"No. But we need a gardener. And Ferdinand comes with Gustav."

"I didn't realize we were moving in the whole

203

Czechoslovakian relief agency."

I stood up and looked over at him. "We aren't. You do remember dinner from last night, don't you?"

He nodded. "It was good. I'll admit it."

I smiled. "The way I figure it, we have about half a person too many. The gardener should come into work half a day, at the most. But, Carter, those two. We can't break 'em up."

"You really like them, don't you?"

"I like Gustav. I think I can learn to like Ferdinand once he gets down off his high horse."

We had finished putting everything back. Carter walked over and pulled me into his arms. "OK. They can stay," he said.

"You're lucky I love you."

"Why's that?"

I looked up. "This was your plan all along. Ain't my fault if you didn't think it through."

Carter pulled back. "I didn't know everyone from Zelda all the way down would quit on us."

"If you'd asked me, I could've told you."

"Is that right?" He leaned in and kissed me.

I didn't even try to answer.

. . .

When we walked into the kitchen from the garage, we found all the staff sitting at the big kitchen table eating. Mrs. Kopek stood up and said, "We no hear, so we eat." Her face was a cross between reproach and regret.

I said, "Have a seat. What's for dinner?"

Remaining standing, she said, "Fish for you. Steak for Mr. Carter."

I put my hat on the counter and said, "Sounds good. Do you mind if we join you?"

Everyone looked at me as if I'd lost my mind. I just kept going. "Mrs. Kopek. Carter. You two sit down. I'll fix our plates." I did just that while Carter helped Mrs. Kopek back to her seat at the far end of the table. He then brought over two extra chairs so we could sit across from each other.

The first course was a mushroom soup. I ladled up a bowl for each of us and brought them to the table, handing off one to Carter who smelled it appreciatively. Everyone else was watching me like I was one of the monkeys at the zoo.

I sat down and said, "Thanks for letting us join you. This is where I ate for the first twelve years of my life and I have lots of good memories here. Ida, can you pass the bread, please?"

The long, tall girl looked around, slightly panicked, but didn't move.

"The bread?" I asked again. I pointed to the basket next to her arm.

She looked at Mrs. Kopek who said something in Czech. Ida picked up the basket and handed it to Ferdinand, who was sitting to my left, and who put it down in front of me. I said, "Thank you."

I took out a piece and, following everyone else's example, I put it on the table. "Here you go, Carter." He grinned as I passed it over to him.

Ferdinand made a comment in Czech. Ida laughed but Nora and Gustav didn't. Mrs. Kopek said something sharp back to him in rebuke.

That was enough for me. "OK, kids. Here's how this is gonna work."

Carter said, "Whoa--"

I raised my hand and shook my head. "Nope. My house. My rules. Ready?" I looked at Mrs. Kopek, who eyes were wide. She just nodded.

"First off, no more Czech. Or Polish. Or German. Or Russian. Just English. Everyone got that?"

They all nodded quietly.

"Second. This isn't the old days. I'm not the King of England and this ain't Buckingham Palace." This made Nora and Gustav laugh. I smiled at Nora. I couldn't see Gustav. He was on the other side of Ferdinand.

"Third. We don't have the kind of lives where we know when we're gonna be home at night. That ain't gonna happen. So, Mrs. Strakova, you cook what you want to cook and, if we're here when it's ready, we'll sit down and eat with you. But if we're not, then we'll eat leftovers. Understand?"

Mrs. Strakova, who was sitting at the head of the table, nodded in obvious relief.

"By the way, we both agree you are a marvelous cook." I pointed at my bowl. "This is the most delicious soup I've ever eaten." I looked around the table. "Don't we all agree?"

Everyone but Ferdinand nodded. I leaned in and said, "You better damn well nod or I'll take you out back and kick your ass."

Carter burst out laughing as did the three other kids. Ferdinand solemnly said, "Yes, Mrs. Strakova, this is the most delicious soup I have ever eaten." He brought his spoon to his mouth and put some in his mouth. After he swallowed, "So delicious. It is the greatest treasure of the Earth." I couldn't see his face, but whatever he was doing made Mrs. Strakova blush hard and pull her apron over her face for a moment.

I leaned in and whispered, "Good job, kid. Thank you."

He whispered back, "You are welcome, Mr. Nick." And he seemed to mean it.

I surveyed the table. Everyone looked much more

relaxed. Mrs. Kopek asked, "No more dinner in dining room?"

I nodded. "Unless we're having guests. I'd rather eat in here."

Carter piped up. "Me, too."

I said, "Since we're laying down the rules, do you have any, Mr. Carter?"

He smiled at me from across the table. "As a matter of fact, Mr. Nick, I do." He looked around at everyone and said, "Don't come into our bedroom when the door is closed. I can't be held responsible for what you might find."

The four kids laughed. Mrs. Kopek and Mrs. Strakova blushed.

. . .

We were in bed, talking about nothing much, when there was a knock on the bedroom door.

Carter said, "I'll get it." He stood up, pulled on his trousers and a shirt. As he did so, there was another knock. "Coming!" Once he was presentable enough, he opened the door.

It was Ferdinand. "The phone. For Mr. Nick." He looked around Carter at me and smiled. It was an odd expression. Smiling wasn't his strong suit.

I said, "Who is it?"

"He didn't say."

Carter said, "When you answer the phone, be sure to ask who is calling."

Ferdinand simply nodded, turned on his heel, and walked away. Carter turned and looked at me. "What's his problem?"

"I think we may have found one human being who isn't automatically in love with you. Welcome to my life." By this time, I was up and pulling on my trousers.

As I grabbed my shirt, he jumped behind me and stuck his fingers between my ribs. Without thinking, I yelped. "Hey!"

"Everyone loves Carter Jones."

I turned and looked at him. He was grinning like a tomcat. "I can't speak for everyone, Mr. Carter, but I certainly do."

He just shook his head. "Knock off the high-hat talk. Just 'cause we're on Nob Hill--"

I stood on my toes and kissed him. That was the best response.

. . .

I picked up the phone and said, "Yeah?"

"Nick, it's Greg."

"Where the hell are you?"

"I'm in Carmel."

"Why?"

"I needed to clear my head. I took a long drive and ended up here. My car transmission died. And I'm stranded. I tried to call Mike, but he's not home." His voice was pitiful.

I looked at my watch. It was just before 11. "Where are you?" I asked.

"At the Hide-A-Way Motel on Highway 1."

"How are you set for cash?"

"That's the deal. I left my wallet at home. I happened to have a ten in my pocket..."

"OK. How much do you have left?"

"About three bucks and some change."

I stood there and thought for a moment. This was either some sort of weird trap to lure me to Carmel. Which made no sense. Carmel? I could see someone luring me to South City or Richmond, but Carmel? Or he was seriously in trouble and had no one to call.

The operator came on the line and said, "Please deposit thirty more cents for another three minutes." I heard the bells ring as Greg did just that.

"Is there a phone in your room?"

"--" He said something but it wasn't clear.

"Greg?"

"Yeah."

"Is there a phone in your room?"

"Yes. Didn't you hear me the first time?"

"No."

"Well, it's real windy--" He cut out again.

I just plowed ahead. "Are you registered under your name?"

"Sure." That was clear.

"OK. Get back there and I'll call you."

"I'm just across--". He cut out again and then the line went dead.

I put the phone back in its cradle. Ferdinand, as he'd done the night before, was standing next to the dining room.

"New rule for you, Ferdinand."

"What?"

"Put on some clothes when you go wandering around the house." He was, once again, padding around in just a pair of drawstring pants.

"Yes, Mr. Nick." He smiled again. It was kind of creepy, truth be told.

I laughed. "Are you really happy or did someone tell you to smile more?"

"Gustav say I should smile more."

I looked at him for a moment. "Is that how you smile at him?"

"No."

"I didn't think so. Ask him to help you practice."

"Yes, Mr. Nick." This was more solemn. Somehow,

that fit him.

"One other rule."

"What?"

"You don't need to wait for me when I'm on the phone."

He nodded and was gone without so much as a "good night."

I picked up the phone and dialed zero.

"Operator."

"Long distance."

"One moment."

I waited as there were several clicks.

Another voice said, "Long distance."

"I'm calling Carmel. Person-to-person from Nick Williams to Greg Holland. The Hide-A-Way Motel on Highway 1."

"One moment."

After a long pause followed by a couple of clicks, the voice returned. "All circuits into Carmel are busy. Shall I try again in five minutes?"

"Thank you." I put the receiver down and wandered into the office. I hadn't really spent any significant time in there since my father had left.

A part of me wanted to snoop in his desk but I knew it was locked. Of course, I could have easily picked the lock and never left any traces, but I decided not to. Instead I just walked around and admired the construction of the room. The walls were paneled, as was the ceiling. It was all beautifully done. I couldn't remember the exact history. I made a mental note to ask my father when he and Lettie got back.

I remembered being constantly curious about that room when I was a kid. And now it was mine. I was free to tap on the walls and finally find the hidden passage door I had been convinced existed.

Just as I was starting to tap on the wall to the left of the door, the phone rang. I ran back into the hall and picked it up.

"Yeah?"

"This is long distance."

"Do you have that call for Carmel?"

"No, sir. I was just informed that the lines between Monterey and San Jose are down because of a windstorm. All lines into Carmel go through Monterey."

"Right. Any idea when they'll be back up?"

"No, sir. Usually these things take a couple of hours to repair."

"Would this affect Western Union?"

"I can connect you but I believe it does."

"Connect me, anyway."

"Yes, sir. My apologies for the inconvenience."

"Well, you didn't knock the poles down yourself, but thank you."

This got a small snicker, which may have been a first.

"Western Union."

"I'm wondering if I can send a telegram to Carmel, California, and when it would arrive."

"One moment."

I waited as several pages were turned.

"We can deliver a telegram after 7 tomorrow morning. Otherwise, it will be called in if you have a phone number for the receiving party at no extra charge."

"The long distance operator just told me the lines between Monterey and San Jose are down because of the wind."

"In that case, the telegram would be delayed. I believe those lines are the same that we use."

"Thank you. I'll try something else."

"Have a good night."

"You, too." I put the phone down and thought about what to do next. I didn't like the idea of making Greg wait, poor guy.

I picked up the phone and tried Mike's number.

"Hello?"

"It's Nick. Where've you been?" I sounded a little more accusatory than I meant to.

"Not that it's any of your business, but I just finished up a long, raging fight with Ray."

"Sorry about that. You OK?"

"Sure."

"Is Ray OK? He's not in the hospital or anything?" I'd been decked by Mike. I wouldn't recommend the experience.

He laughed. "No. He's probably drowning his sorrows."

"What happened?"

"Well, he was--"

I interrupted him. "Sorry, Mike. Tell me later."

"Sure." He was irritated.

"Greg called me a few minutes ago."

"He did?"

"Yeah. He's stranded in Carmel. He was on a payphone. I told him I'd call him back in his motel room but then the lines went down and now there's no way to call him or send a telegram. Not for a couple of hours, at least."

"Oh, Nick." I could hear the exasperation in his voice. "I know what you want to do but it's three hours down there." He sighed. "And three hours back."

"Then get some coffee to go at that diner by your building and meet me at the corner in front. I'll be by in about ten minutes to pick you up."

He sighed again. "Fine."

I put down the phone.

. . .

Carter was driving. He had insisted on going. We were waiting for Mike to get another cup of coffee for him. And some sandwiches.

"What if this is a trap?" he asked as Beethoven was playing on the car radio.

"I thought about that. But... Carmel? A trap?"

"Well, it's the end of the road."

"If you don't count Big Sur."

"Still." He tapped his fingers on the steering wheel and looked at me. In the light of the diner's windows, I could see his forehead was wrinkled with worry.

"I can see being lured to an empty warehouse in Dogpatch. But Carmel?"

Just then, Mike got in behind me and slammed the door closed. "Damn, it's windy out there. Let's get this rocket ship going."

. . .

By the time we were on Potrero, Mike was finished with his sandwich. I knew this because he was rolling down his window. Over his shoulder, Carter said, "Just throw your trash in the floorboard." Mike didn't say anything but he did roll up his window.

I turned around and looked at him. "So, what happened with Ray?"

"Well, I guess I know why I had a bad feeling about him."

"What?" asked Carter.

"He went to confession."

"And?" I asked.

"His priest told him to repent. And so he is."

Carter said, "Well, good for him."

213

"This is what you two fought about?"

Mike sat back and crossed his arms. "What we fought about was the fact that he wants to go back to work for the City."

Carter said, "Well, shit."

Mike nodded. "Not that they'll have him."

Carter said, "They might. He was good."

We sat there in silence for a moment. I could feel the car speed up. I turned and noticed we were now on the Bayshore Freeway. I looked at the speedometer and saw that Carter was now pegging 70.

"OK, speed demon."

Mike leaned forward and said, "You're fine. There's a construction zone further south. But this part is done."

I noticed that the new six-lane road was smooth and perfect. The car, however, was moving around a bit.

"Still windy?" I asked.

"Yeah," was Carter's terse reply.

I turned back to look at Mike and asked, "What did you say to him?"

"I reminded him what happened when he turned his back on his true nature before."

"When he got married?"

"Right. I told him to really think about it. He told me he had thought about it. I asked him if he was thinking about it the last time I fucked him 'cause he didn't act like he was thinking about anything else but me right then. He had no comment."

Carter and I both burst out laughing.

Chapter 19

Standard Gas Station
N. Main at E. Laurel
Salinas, Cal.
Thursday, June 24, 1954
Half past 2 in the morning

The wind was so strong that I had to hold on to my hat as I walked back to the car after using the restroom in the back of the service station. We had plenty of gas, but decided to fill up at the all-night station in the middle of Salinas and use their facilities. They didn't sell coffee, but they had a Coke machine and I grabbed one for each of us.

Once we were all back in the car, Carter pulled out back onto Main Street. We were watching for the turn-off to Monterey. After a couple of blocks, I pointed at the sign. As Carter made that right, he said, "I think we're being followed."

Mike asked, "What makes you think that?"

"There's a black Mercury 8 that I've seen several

times. First was when we got on the Bayshore Freeway. It was about ten car lengths behind us. After we were on the south side of San Jose, I noticed it again. It just followed us at the turn-off. Might be a coincidence, but I'm pretty sure I saw it parked behind the Standard station when I went to the bathroom."

Mike said, "How fast you going?"

"About 45."

"Slowly speed up to 60. Then slow back down to 45. Do it like you're not paying attention. Watch what the other driver does. And, Nick, don't turn around."

Carter did what Mike suggested. "He sped up and slowed down in tandem."

Mike asked, "Who do you think it is?"

I said, "The Keller brothers."

Mike said, "Yep. You bring a gun?"

I opened the glove box and pulled out the revolver I had stashed there the Thursday before. "I have my revolver." I looked at it. "It's loaded."

I could hear Mike eject the cartridge on his pistol. "Mine, too." He inserted the cartridge again.

. . .

We were about halfway to Monterey when we came to a spot in the highway that was a flat straightaway which curved sharply to the right and narrowed as it passed through two hills. Mike said, "See that?"

Carter said, "Yeah." I heard the transmission purr as he put his foot down on the gas pedal.

I said, "This is a straight eight. That Mercury can outrun us."

"I know."

I couldn't help it. I turned around and saw the lights of the car behind us getting closer. I turned forward, put my hand on the dashboard, and watched as the

216

curve approached.

As Carter began to turn into the curve, I saw something bright jump out in front of our Buick. It was a deer. I sucked in my breath.

Reacting instinctively, Carter slammed on the brakes and the car began to skid on the concrete road. Carter turned into the skid and managed to quickly straighten us out but, by this time, the Mercury was right on us. It rammed the back of our car.

I saw Carter put his foot all the way down but the Mercury stayed right on us. We were now on another straightaway. The Mercury came around on our left and slammed into the rear of the car.

I heard the crash of metal and glass. Carter moved over to the right and let the Mercury come up about halfway. He turned the steering wheel sharply to the left as it came up on the passenger door.

There was an awful scraping sound. The Mercury's chrome bumper was pushing into the side of our car. The driver moved over to the left. Carter said, "Hold on!" He pressed down hard on the brake, causing the Mercury to shoot past us. He sped back up and began to weave back and forth on the highway, making it difficult for the other driver to do the same thing to us. The Mercury sped up.

We passed a sign that said we were five miles out of Monterey. I could see a brightness reflected by the cloudy sky that confirmed we were almost there.

Soon the Mercury's tail lights were gone. After a couple of miles, we came to another curve, this one to the left. As Carter turned the wheel, I could see something shiny on the roadway that was illuminated by our headlights. Big pieces of sharp metal, like shrapnel, were scattered across the concrete surface of the road.

Before any words came out of my mouth, Carter swerved onto the rough shoulder. The car shook and bumped as we drove over gravel and shrub. I heard a big pop and the car began to wobble. I didn't know which one, but one of the passenger-side tires had blown out. Carter brought the car to a quick stop. As he did so, he turned off the engine and killed the lights.

Mike said, "Roll down your windows about two inches."

We both did this as Mike did the same in the backseat. The wind was strong, cold, and tangy. We were close to the ocean, that was for sure. It was also whistling.

"Down a little more until the sound stops." We did that.

As we sat there, we listened. My gun was ready. Mike quietly asked, "Can you disable the dashboard lamp?"

Carter reached over, banged off the cover, and forcibly pulled out the bulb. I knew there was a button somewhere, but that was simpler.

"Slump down below the window level." We did that. "Nick, slowly open your door but don't get out. Let's see what happens when you do that."

I pulled on the handle and let gravity do the work. The car was on a slight incline to the right from the blowout. The door swung open on its own weight.

From behind us, a bullet shot out. It didn't sound like it hit the car. I whispered, "Sloppy."

"Yeah." That was Mike.

"Good." That was Carter.

Mike opened the door behind mine and let it swing out. Two more shots rang out. I definitely heard one of the bullets hit a rock. The twing sound was distinctive. The other one hit something, but it wasn't our car.

"What now?" asked Carter.

"We listen and we wait."

As we sat there, I could hear the wind whistling through the trees on our side of the road. In the faintly reflected light, I could see that the trees were on the side of an embankment that was probably twenty or thirty feet high. I saw something blink in the sky. I wondered what it was until it happened again.

"The airport is over that ridge. I'm seeing the white and green lamp flash on the right."

Mike said, "Here's what we do. You two noisily walk up the hill--"

Carter hissed, "Noisily?"

"They're lousy shots. You just need to let them know you're on the move. Stay low and you'll be fine."

"What about you?" I asked.

"I'm gonna wait and, as they pass by, and they will, I'm gonna pop 'em."

"You sure about that?" I whispered.

"Yes. Go."

Carter slid over next to me as I fell out of the car and began to make my way up the side of the hill. As I did so, I said, "Come on." And I said it loudly. Sure enough, several random bullets flew through the air. None of them were anywhere close.

As we moved in a diagonal away from the car and up the hill, Carter replied, "OK," which launched another volley of shots. When we got to the crest of the hill, I pulled Carter down flat and we watched.

Sure enough, two figures were walking along the side of the road and were about twenty feet behind the car. I reached for a rock and put it in Carter's hand. Then I grabbed one of my own and threw it towards the road. Carter followed my lead. As we watched, one of the guys began to wildly shoot until his gun was empty. The other said, "Damn it," and loudly. They were walking along the right side of the car when there were two loud pops and a whole lot of screaming and cursing. Mike had gotten them both in the legs.

We scrambled down the side of the hill. Mike had picked up both their guns and was searching them. He tossed me their billfolds as he found them. I said to Carter, "Take off your tie," as I began to pull mine off.

Mike used our ties to bind the men's arms. They weren't gonna be walking anywhere. Carter had a bag of clothes from the gymnasium in the trunk. He'd managed to go to Ike's place a couple of times since the fire. We used his t-shirts as tourniquets to help stop the bleeding from the gunshots. We also put their feet up, which would help as well.

Mike asked, "Where's your car?"

Vernon Keller spat out, "Not gonna tell you, faggot."

Mike shook his head. "If you wanna bleed out, that's fine with me. But, thanks to you, this car isn't--"

Randolph Keller, the egghead who'd built the secret mechanism for our safe in the basement, moaned and said, "It's about 200 feet back, pulled off. Just past the shrapnel."

"Thanks." Mike, who already had the keys, sprinted off to get the car. I reached into the glove box and pulled out a flashlight. I clicked it on and shined it in Vernon Keller's face.

"Who torched our house?"

"I don't know what you mean, faggot."

Carter walked over, put his feet on either side of Keller and squatted down. "You want to rethink that answer?"

"You can't do anything to me. You're not a cop."

Carter pulled back and smacked the guy hard on the face. "You're right. I'm not a cop. I'm an aggrieved citizen whose house fucking burned to the ground

220

thanks to you."

Keller tried to spit up at Carter. Gravity didn't help. Carter pulled back and hit him again. Not quite as hard this time, but still...

The egghead said, "Vern, you're a fucking idiot. Of course, we did it."

"Where's my Peacemaker?" I asked. I shined the flashlight on him. His nervous tic was happening so fast, it was contorting the left side of his face and beginning to look like a palsy.

The egghead replied, "At the bottom of the bay. I threw it and the bullets off the Bay Bridge last night."

"Why'd you kill Rutledge?" I asked.

Mike pulled up right then. I walked over and opened the passenger door. I said, "Go get help. I don't think it's safe to move them. Do you?" I was feeling vengeful right then, so it probably wasn't the best move. Mike smirked and nodded. I shut the door. The tires squealed on the pavement as he sped off.

I walked back over to the two clowns on the side of the road. The wind was cold and blowing hard but I hardly noticed. "I figure you have about fifteen minutes to make a very important decision. Either you tell us everything." I made a point of looking at my watch, which I couldn't see in the dark. "And you start in the next minute. Or we remove those tourniquets and let you bleed out. Your choice."

Carter stood up and kicked Vernon's leg close to but not on the bullet wound. The man howled.

The egghead said, "I'll tell you everything, man."

I nodded as Carter walked over next to me. I pulled out my revolver and pointed it. "Go ahead."

"It was all Vern's idea. He wanted to start his own mob. To compete with Abati."

I laughed and then said, "Go on."

"I told him I knew where we could get the cash to bankroll things."

In frustration, I shot the gun above the man's head. The bullet went into an otherwise innocent tree.

Carter said, "Nick!"

"Better that poor tree than one of these guys. Go on."

The aroma of urine floated up in the air from where the two brothers were laid out. I felt bad. But not that bad.

The egghead said, "Vern knew he was being squeezed out of Universal when that guy from Connecticut arrived. So, we decided to murder Russell and try to somehow pin the blame on you or on Abati."

I said, "Too bad there isn't a mobster school."

"Yeah, we should've left his body up on the top floor."

"So you planned on killing Russell and then skimmed the payoff after inflating the amount to also get more outta Henry?"

"That was Vern's stupid idea. I told him the newsprint idea was idiotic. But, no, he's gotta be a fancy-ass mobster."

"Shut the fuck up, Randy."

Carter walked over to the trunk and grabbed something. In the dark, it looked like a sock. He walked over to Vernon and stuffed it in the guy's mouth. He made a big fuss until Carter kicked him again.

"Go on." That was Carter as he walked back over to where I was standing.

"Then I called Henry Winters to threaten him. You had talked to both of us, so we couldn't call you. But Winters hadn't heard my voice. Using the money from Universal's payoff, we hired a couple of blockheads." Vernon started making a noise again. "They were supposed to just tail you and let us know. I dunno why they decided to break and enter. That wasn't what we told them to do. What did they tell the cops?"

"I haven't heard. Must not have been much. Probably too embarrassed. How did they know my father's name?"

"I gave them a dossier."

I laughed. "In writing?"

"Sure. Why?"

"Well, I'm not gonna give you tips on how to be a better mobster, if that's what you're thinking. Then what?"

"The next night we broke into your house and went through your stuff. That's when I found the Peacemaker. And the bullets. I thought that was a nice touch."

Carter growled, "I'd move on, if you don't want another bullet in you. I'll do it myself."

He swallowed. "Yeah, OK. While we were there, I opened the safe."

I asked, "How'd you know the combination?"

"You never changed it. I had cracked it when I was installing the--" He was interrupted when I shot off two more bullets into another innocent tree.

"Sorry. Gun just went off."

"Um, yeah." He had already emptied his bladder. I hoped he could hold everything else in until an ambulance arrived. "So, we poured gasoline over everything."

"How many gallons did you use?" asked Carter.

"Five."

"Overkill."

"Remember, Chief, this isn't a mission report. Then what?"

"We laid low over the weekend. Then, early Monday morning Vern stupidly went to Rutledge to try to shake him down."

I wanted to mention how the silver bullet was a dead giveaway, but I decided not to.

"What about Lysander Blythe?"

"That was all Vern." His brother began to fidget and make noise again. "He went over and threatened to torch their house unless the guy copped to doing it himself. Truth is, I don't know why the poor guy agreed to do it. Vern isn't that scary."

This really pissed his brother off. Carter walked over and kicked him one more time.

I asked, "Then Vernon strangled him when the police wouldn't believe him and left his body on the porch?"

"Yeah."

I couldn't help myself. "Sloppy."

In the fifteen or so minutes that we'd been standing there, the wind had died down somewhat. No one had passed in either direction. Suddenly, I could hear a car coming from Salinas and realized there was still shrapnel in the road. I handed my gun to Carter and ran down the highway waving my arms like a damn fool while Carter called after me to stop.

Epilogue

Hide-A-Way Motel
Highway 1
Carmel-by-the-Sea, Cal.
Thursday, June 24, 1954
Just past 10 in the morning

It took a while to get everything straightened out at the police station in Monterey. We each had to give sworn statements. And then Mike and I helped the sergeant interview the Keller brothers. Vernon wouldn't stop screaming at his brother, so they finally put him a holding cell while the sergeant finished running down Randolph's story. He provided more details, but his story was basically the same.

It was just past 10 when our cab pulled in front of the Hide-A-Way Motel. Carter and I waited outside while Mike asked for Greg's room. We weren't sure he would even be there. None of us had thought to call him from the police station.

Mike walked out, smiling, and motioned us to follow

225

him. As we walked down the row of rooms, I saw a familiar brand-new '54 Cadillac parked in front of Room 7. I nudged Carter, who nodded, but neither of us said anything. No one wants kids to interrupt a honeymoon, or second honeymoon, or whatever it was.

When we got to Room 11, Mike knocked on the door. Greg Holland, looking clean and spiffy, like he'd just gotten out of the shower opened the door. When he saw that it was us, he slammed the door closed.

I moved Mike over and said, "Greg. Let us in. We left right after you called. But then we got run off the road. We just got back from the police station."

The door opened. "Yeah?" He looked at me darkly.

Mike reached above my head and pushed the door open."Yes."

Carter muscled in and pushed me forward, making Greg back up. "When my husband tells you something, you'd better believe him. None of us have had any sleep. We came down here at midnight to save your sorry ass. Now, sit down and let Mike tell you all about it. Then you two make out, or whatever. Meanwhile, Nick and I are gonna get a room and make some phone calls and do unnatural things. Got it?"

Greg was laughing by this time and just nodded his head. Mike walked over, leaned down, put his hands around Greg's head, and began to seriously make out with the man. It was real sweet.

. . .

Once we were checked into Room 22, I got on the horn and called the office.

"Nick! Where are you? Mrs. Kopek is frantic. Henry has called three times. What's going on?" It was Marnie.

I briefly explained the situation. "We'll spend the

226

night here and come back in the morning. Would you call Mrs. Kopek and tell her?

"Sure."

"Have you heard from your mother?"

"She sent a telegram this morning. They're down there in Carmel."

"I know. We saw my father's car in the parking lot here at the Hide-A-Way Motel."

"Are you gonna let them know you're there?"

"No. I don't wanna interrupt their trip."

"Mother won't like that."

"What she doesn't know--"

"Nick! I can't lie to Mother."

"Really? Does she know that you and Alex are already shacked up?"

"Nick! You wouldn't! You're the meanest brother ever!"

I laughed. "How long have you been waiting to use that line?"

"Since Christmas."

. . .

"Henry, it's Nick."

"Where are you?"

"Carmel. Long story. What's up?"

"Abati's men have leaned on me, again."

"What do they want?"

"The payoff for the concrete that we never gave Russell."

"How much?"

"Two grand."

"Fine. You have it?"

"Yes, but--"

"Just go get it and pay them off. Cost of doing business. I'll reimburse you, like I said I would before."

"You sure?"

"Yeah. Just make sure to get it in hundreds and write down the serial numbers. That's just good backup."

"Right. When will you be back?"

"Tomorrow sometime. We'll meet up in the next couple of days and I'll tell you what's happened. Here's the bottom line. We know who killed Russell and Rutledge and torched the house." I didn't think he knew about Lysander Blythe and that wasn't the time.

"Was it Vernon Keller?"

"Yeah. How'd you know?"

"He's the only connection."

"That's right. You ever get tired of engineering and project management, you can come work for me."

"I'll stick to what I know, but thanks for the offer."

. . .

After some rolling around in the hay, a long nap, and a longer shower, we got dressed and went out for an early dinner. The fog was thick and it was chilly.

As the cab was taking us to a restaurant the owner of the motel had suggested, we passed a Mercury dealership. I said, "Stop here."

The guy pulled over, I threw him a five, and we got out. We walked the half a block to the small showroom. I wondered if they had any cars in stock or if they had them shipped in on order, like in the old days.

We walked in and a short, stout blonde man walked up. "Can I help you gentlemen?"

Carter said, "I'm looking for a--" I pulled on his coat sleeve and pointed. Right in the middle of the circular showroom was a vanilla convertible. The seats were covered in a beautiful saddle leather. We walked over there and just looked at it.

Without saying a word, the salesman opened the

door, reached down, pushed the seat back, and then gestured. Carter got in and put his hands on the steering wheel.

"It's a V-8. Three speed manual. You can add--"

"Sold," said Carter.

I laughed as the man looked at Carter and then at me. "Should we take a test drive?"

Carter jumped out, slammed the door closed, and said, "No, sir. Just show me where to sign. My banker here will write you a check."

I smiled and nodded as the bewildered man said, "Let me talk to my manager. One moment." He walked off shaking his head.

"Really?" I asked.

"Really."

"You don't want to--"

"When have you ever taken a car for a test drive?"

I shrugged. "Never. But that's me. Spending..." I looked at the invoice. "Just under three grand is a big leap for you."

Carter looked down at me. "I learned from the master."

I shrugged. "Who am I to argue?"

. . .

An hour later, Carter pulled the Mercury into the last spot in the small parking lot next to a building that was barely more than a shack. The place was called Giuseppe's and was supposed to have good Italian dishes. Carter, on his way to finally letting garlic be a part of his life, had agreed after I promised I would taste the sauce first.

We walked in and were greeted by a dark-haired woman of about 40. "Welcome to Giuseppe's. For dinner?"

I nodded. "Just the two of us."

She smiled and said, "Five minutes, please." The place didn't have a bar, so we waited in the corner by the door. I looked around. The place was very cozy. The tables were covered in red-and-white checkered tablecloths and there were candles on each table. The aromas from the kitchen were tantalizing. I was looking forward to a big dinner and then getting to bed early. And that's when I saw my father and Lettie. They were seated at a table in the back, drinking red wine, and laughing about something.

I whispered to Carter, "They're here. What do you want to do?"

He glanced at the table and said, "They look like they're having fun." He smiled. "Too late."

I looked and Lettie was motioning us over. My father was smiling. We made our way to their table.

"Hello, boys. This is a nice surprise." Lettie's voice was warm and inviting. My father stood up to shake Carter's hand and then mine.

I said, "We're actually staying at the Hide-A-Way but didn't want to bother you."

My father smiled. "That was very considerate of you, Nicholas." He looked around for the waiter, who walked over. "This is my son and his friend. Can you bring us two chairs so they can join us?"

The man nodded. "Of course." He brought over the chairs and, after moving a few things around, we all sat down.

"So," began Lettie, "What brings you two down here?"

I said, "Let's get some beer and then we'll tell you all about it."

The evening stretched into several hours as we gave them a few of the highlights of our adventures and heard all about theirs. They had arrived in Carmel on Monday evening and decided they didn't want to go any further. My father told us that he was thinking about buying a ranch south of town. They had already been to see it and Lettie was in love with the place. The house was modern and had a panoramic view of the ocean. I had a feeling we might be coming down a lot.

As we were eating, I asked, "But, Lettie, I thought you didn't like staying hotels?"

My father cocked his head to the side and asked, "Is that true, Leticia?"

She smiled and said, "You are correct, Nicholas. I don't like hotels. Not one bit. But a motel..."

For some reason, my father blushed. Carter stifled a laugh and I quickly changed the subject. Whatever it was, I didn't want to know.

. . .

We told them about our all-Czechoslovakian staff. Lettie was enchanted with the idea. My father was very... tolerant. I figured once he saw what was happening, he might have a few opinions to get off his chest.

My father insisted on paying for dinner, so I let him. It was the first time I'd been to a restaurant with my father that I could remember. When I noticed how small the tip was, I couldn't help but drop an extra twenty on the table as my father was helping Lettie into her coat. Carter noticed and smiled in a way that made me feel nice and warm inside.

We went outside to the small parking lot and showed off Carter's new car. He was just as proud of it as if it was a baby. At one point he mentioned it was only the second car he'd ever bought. I knew about the first one, an old Ford he and Henry had driven across the

231

country to get to San Francisco. But I had never thought about how he hadn't had one since selling that one for fifty bucks. When my father heard that amount, he laughed and said he thought the dealer was being generous.

. . .

Before going back to the motel, we drove over to a spot overlooking the ocean and sat there with the engine running and the heater blowing. We had put the top down and I was sitting in the crook of Carter's arm.

"That was one of the best meals I can ever remember having."

I nodded and said, "I agree." I sighed. "They're so much in love."

"Yes. And they belong here."

I sighed. "Just like we belong in that big pile of rocks."

Carter squeezed me, leaned over, and kissed me deeply until it got too cold.

. . .

Before we left Carmel the next morning, we went to the Monterey police impound lot. The Buick was being held as evidence. I had called the local dealer and asked if one of their mechanics could meet us there.

Once the man got a good look at the damage, he said, "The frame is bent. I'd be happy to repair it for you, but you're just wasting your dough."

I couldn't say anything. Carter said, "You want it for parts?"

"Nah. Not us. But I have a cousin who would. He can strip it and junk it. Probably give you fifty bucks for it."

Carter handed the man a hundred. "If you could take care of that for us, we'd appreciate it."

The guy's eyes popped when he looked at the bill. "Sure thing, Mister."

I could feel my eyes getting wet. I was going to miss that car.

. . .

Carter pulled the Mercury to the curb on Van Ness in front of McAlister's Buick.

"What are we doing here?"

"Getting you a new car."

I looked at my watch.

Carter said, "We have plenty of time. They don't get in until 8." We were meeting Aunt Velma and Mrs. Jones at the airport.

I nodded. "OK."

Once we were inside, my eye was drawn to a car I'd never seen before. I walked over and looked at it. It was a big '54 Roadmaster convertible coupe. The body was red and the cover was white. The hood had a snub nose and the trunk was squared off. I liked the look of the beast.

"Is this it?" asked Carter.

I nodded. "I was thinking about a Skylark, but it would always remind me of Janet. Besides, they're not that powerful."

"Why not a Super?"

"Not yet."

. . .

We were standing next to the Mercury as *The Laconic Lumberjack* rolled up and parked about two hundred feet from us. The sun was setting and the sky was full of long streaks of cloud colored with pink and orange and purple. It wasn't warm, but it wasn't cold, either.

I was glad Aunt Velma and Mrs. Jones had wanted to

wait a day to get things together before they left. Otherwise, Marnie would've had to pick them up the night before while we were in Carmel. I was honestly looking forward to seeing them both.

Once the propellers had stopped, a couple of men in blue coveralls rolled a portable stairway in front of the plane's door. I saw Captain Morris salute us from the cockpit window. I smiled and waved in return.

As soon as the stairs were in place, we walked over to the bottom and waited. One of the men bounded up and knocked on the airplane door. We started up the steps as he walked down. Christine, the stewardess and wife of the captain, opened the door. She said, "Hello, Mr. Williams. Mr. Jones."

I smiled. "Hello, Christine. Good flight?"

"Yes. And I so enjoyed getting to know our passengers. The day just flew by. Seems like we just left."

We followed her in. Aunt Velma and Mrs. Jones were waiting for us. We exchanged hugs with Aunt Velma. Carter got a kiss on the cheek from his mother. I got a nice handshake from her gloved hand.

Once we were down the stairs and loading the Mercury, Mrs. Jones asked, "Is this a new car?"

I smiled. "It's Carter's. He finally bought one."

She nodded but didn't say anything. I wondered if this had been a good idea.

. . .

The drive home was fine enough. Carter drove, Aunt Velma and I talked, and Mrs. Jones said very little.

As we pulled into the garage, Mrs. Jones said, "This is such a large house."

Carter said, "It is, Mama. I think you'll like it."

There was no response.

. . .

It was nearly 9 in the evening when we walked into the kitchen. Gustav came in from the dining room. He was wearing his oddly tailored morning suit. We made introductions.

Aunt Velma looked around and said, "I think this is bigger than our kitchen at home, don't you agree, Louise?"

Mrs. Jones looked around and said, "I really couldn't say."

I glanced at Carter, who looked disappointed.

. . .

Gustav and Ferdinand brought in their luggage. Mrs. Kopek and Nora showed them their rooms on the third floor and helped them both unpack.

Carter and I, meanwhile, sat in the great room.

"Do you want a fire?" I asked.

Carter shook his head. He stood up and walked over to the double doors that led out to the garden and opened them up. "Stuffy in here."

"Nervous?" I asked.

He turned on me. "This is your fault. I would've told you not to do this." He crossed his arms and stood there, glowering in the light of the floor lamp.

I stood up and walked over. "I'm sorry." I didn't know what else to say.

He relaxed. "I know you meant well."

I reached up and kissed him on the cheek. He didn't smile.

"Nothing?" I asked.

He sighed and kept his arms crossed.

"Is this about sleeping with me in the same house as your mother?"

He furrowed his brow and nodded slowly. "Yeah."

"I understand."

"Yeah. I guess you do at that."

Right then, I could hear the sounds of several people coming down the stairs. We could hear them talking as they did.

"Yes. I tell my Ivan that I don't care who he love. I only want him be happy." That was Mrs. Kopek.

I looked at Carter, who was blushing intensely.

"Well, I don't know--" That was Mrs. Jones.

"Louise. What's done is done. It's time for you to realize how lucky you are." That was Aunt Velma.

"I have to get used to it, is all. I'm here, aren't I?"

As they came into the great room, Mrs. Kopek said, "That is most important of all."

Carter walked over to his mother, nervously put his hands in his pockets, and said, "She's right, Mama. That's the most important thing of all."

I could hear the emotion in his voice. She looked up at him for a long moment. Finally, she opened her arms and said, "Just give me time."

Carter hugged her and said, "As long as it takes, Mama."

My eyes were getting wet again.

. . .

On the following Monday, I met with Kenneth Wilcox. He was my lawyer. Until April, his offices had been on the fourth floor of our building on Bush Street. But, his operation got too big for the cramped space so he was now over on Pine in a small office building I'd bought. Once the building on Market was done, they would move in there with the rest of us.

"Are you sure you want to do this?" Kenneth was sitting behind his desk. His face was wrinkled with concern.

"Yeah. Why?"

He shrugged. "I just never saw you as the kind of guy who would own a construction company."

I smiled. "That's the whole point. I won't."

"But, you will. You'll own fifty-one percent."

I waved away his concern. "That's just to start. I doubt I'll own any of it after a few years. What did their lawyer say?"

"The board is happy to sell. Without Thomas Rutledge, there's no one qualified to run it."

"What about Troyer? Did you make it clear that retaining him was a condition of the sale?"

Kenneth nodded. "Sure. That was fine. You got everything you wanted."

I looked out the grimy window of his small office and thought about Rutledge and his senseless death. "I guess so."

. . .

I walked back down to Bush after I left Kenneth's office. When I opened the door to the office, Mike and Ben were waiting for me.

I put my hat on the rack and sat down at my desk.

"What's up?" I asked.

Mike leaned forward. "Since Carter and Martinelli are down in Gilroy today, I had a short meeting with Ray first thing."

"You? How'd it go?"

"Lasted five minutes. He gave me his keys and his forwarding address." He leaned back and sighed. "His ex-wife's house. They're getting back together."

"Sorry about that, Mike."

"Yeah. Well, that's done."

"Did he say anything about going back to work for

the City?"

"Said that he had a meeting set up with his captain today. I told him good luck and I meant it."

I nodded. "Yeah. I hope it turns out OK for him." That reminded me of Jeffery. I wondered what he was doing right then.

But, before I could think too much about him, Mike said, "Also wanted to let you know that the Keller brothers have been transported here. You, Carter, and me will probably have to be interviewed by the new man in charge of the case at Central. Straight arrow by the name of Lieutenant George Bruhn."

I smiled. "Straight arrow?"

Ben nodded. "Oh, yeah. By the books. Hard nose."

Mike smiled at me. "I met with him this morning. His blue tie had a dried mustard stain on it."

I laughed. "So, he's not one of us?"

Ben looked confused. "He's married. Got two daughters."

Mike turned to the kid and said, "I'll explain later."

I looked at Ben. "What about Vernon Keller? You ever remember what that was?"

He nodded. "Yeah. It was the last name."

Mike said, "His brother, Randolph Keller, your safe guy. He'd been up at Folsom for insurance fraud."

"Fraud?" I asked. "Why Folsom?"

"He made out with a hundred thousand. Back in '42." That was impressive.

"How much time did he do?"

"Eight years."

Ben said, "I knew the name because when I did a stint in the probation office, he was on my roster."

I nodded. "So, he'd just been released a year when I hired him."

Marnie piped up. "I hired him, Nick. Remember? He

was a friend of my cousin, Charlene."

I looked around Mike at Marnie who was standing in the doorway. "Have you told your cousin yet?"

"Yeah. She don't believe me. That's my pop's side of the family. They're all a little crazy."

. . .

On Thursday night, Carter and I stood in front of our old house and looked at it for a long moment. During the daytime, a crew was at work clearing out the debris. It was hard to watch it slowly disappearing, but it was.

I said, "I'll come over tomorrow and start looking through the pile of what they've set aside." The crew was pulling out things they thought might be salvageable. The one problem was that we had to go through them. Since Carter had done a lot of that already, I'd volunteered to do the next round. It was hard work. And that had nothing to do with any sort of manual labor.

I heard the door open at Pam and Diane's house. "Yoo hoo!" That was Diane.

We crossed over to their house and walked up the front steps. Diane gave me a big hug and said, "It's good to see you both."

I replied, "Good to see you, too."

Carter leaned down and gave Diane a kiss on the cheek. She smiled and led us inside.

Evelyn, our friend who lived on the other side of Pam and Diane, was in their sitting room along with her girlfriend, Mary. We said hello and exchanged hugs and handshakes.

Evelyn asked, "Isn't your mother in town?"

Carter nodded.

By way of explanation to Mary, I said, "Mrs. Jones is

here with Carter's Aunt Velma. They went on a sightseeing tour today with Marnie and her squeeze Alex. They're taking in a movie tonight."

"What are they seeing?" asked Mary.

I smiled. "They wanted to see the Fox Theater. So, it's whatever's playing there."

"How's the visit been?" asked Evelyn.

Carter answered before I could say anything. "Fine." His voice was short and curt. I couldn't blame him. It hadn't been an easy time either of them. I had forgotten how stubborn they both could be.

I added, "I asked Aunt Velma to help get the new staff settled in. She's also been working with the interior decorator to update some of the rooms. I think she and Mrs. Kopek have become fast friends..." I felt like I was talking about a country house in England. It was odd. Then I remembered the most important thing. "We also got a new box of red plum jam."

"What's that?" asked Mary.

Evelyn said, "It's the best jam you'll ever taste. Carter's mother makes some every year. Aren't the trees in her own backyard?"

Carter nodded but didn't say anything. I reached over and took his hand. He squeezed it.

I asked, "Where's Pam?"

Diane replied, "She's still upstairs. She only got home about twenty minutes ago." Crossing her arms, she asked, "What is this all about?"

I said, "It's a secret. It'll have to wait until Pam gets down here."

Diane looked at me sideways for a moment and then smiled. "Who wants deviled eggs?"

. . .

Once we were all seated at the dining room table and

tucked in with dinner, I asked, "Pam?"

She looked up from her chicken divan. "What?"

"I'm gonna ask you something but you have to promise not to get upset."

She put down her fork and looked at Diane, who smiled. "What?"

"Promise not to get upset?"

"What, Nick?"

"Promise?"

"Damn it! I promise. Now, what the hell is it?"

Out of the corner of my eye, I saw Mary look over at Evelyn with a worried expression. I tried very hard not to smile.

"I need you to do me a favor."

Pam rolled her eyes. "For chrissakes, what is it?"

"I'm gonna buy Universal Construction and I want you to run it."

Pam sat back in her chair. "What?"

Diane looked at me. "Are you serious, Nick?"

I nodded.

Carter said, "That's not all."

Evelyn asked, "What else?"

I looked at Pam. "I want to give you a forty-nine percent stake." Diane gasped. Pam just sat there, looking at her plate.

I sat there and let it sink in. After a moment, I added, "And then, when you have the cash, you can buy me out. If you want."

Mary's eyes were wide. "A woman running a construction company?" She put her hand to her mouth and looked around the table.

This seemed to get to Pam. She sat up and looked right at me. "Damn straight. Men are idiots. Everybody knows that."

We all laughed.

. . .

After dinner, we gathered in their sitting room. It was stuffed with all sorts of furniture and none of it matched. The one thing it all had in common, however, was that every piece was comfortable. I liked that.

Pam asked, "What happened to all that money of yours?"

Diane was scandalized. "Pam!"

I smiled. "We got it back. Minus about a hundred bucks. It was in their car."

"Did you ever figure out who was leaning on Rutledge to do the stop-work?" asked Pam.

"It was Vernon Keller. It was part of his plan to be a mobster. I don't know why Rutledge fell for it. Keller's brother was the real brains but everything Vernon did was sloppy."

Carter added, "Fortunately for us, neither of them could shoot a gun."

I grinned. "Yeah."

Evelyn said, "What I want to know is what's gonna happen with Vivienne Blythe."

I asked, "Have any of you talked to her since her husband was murdered?"

Diane nodded. "I saw her this morning when I was on my way home from shopping. She invited me in for a cup of tea."

"How's she doing?" asked Mary.

"Well, you can imagine." She leaned against Pam who put her arm around her shoulder. "She's taking it hard but putting on a brave face. She told me she's going to sell and move back east."

Evelyn asked me, "And you're certain who the killer was?"

I nodded. "Yeah. The cops down in Carmel got his

brother's full confession. Once the brother told all, Vernon broke down and admitted everything. There's not going to be a trial. The sentencing hearing should be in a couple of weeks, from what I heard."

Mary asked, "What's the punishment?"

I smiled grimly. "Vernon Keller will get the gas chamber in San Quentin. No question. Murder, arson, conspiracy, theft. His brother might get life since he confessed and cooperated."

The room went quiet for a while. Finally, Evelyn asked Diane, "Did Mrs. Blythe say anything about the play her husband was writing about Nick?"

Diane nodded. "She said she threw the thing in the fire."

. . .

That Sunday was the fourth of July. We went out on *The Flirtatious Captain* to celebrate. My father and Lettie were back and came out with us. Aunt Velma and Carter's mother were in the lounge with them along with Marnie and her boyfriend, Alex. Mrs. Kopek and Mrs. Strakova, who had brought several trays of sandwiches for lunch along with cases of beer and soda pop, were in there as well.

Carter and I were sitting on the forward-facing bench on the top deck.

Ike and Sam were sitting to my right. Gustav, Ferdinand, Ida, and Nora were all squeezed onto the bench facing us. From what I could tell, the four kids were trying to bring Sam up to date on the latest Czech slang. And he was trying to teach it to Ike. Apparently Ike was mangling his Czech and the kids thought this was hilarious.

Dawson and Andy were sitting on the bench on Carter's left. They weren't saying a lot. Andy had his

243

arm around Dawson and they were having fun listening to the Czech antics while taking in the view.

Henry and Robert couldn't come because they had decided to take a long weekend trip to L.A. That was also where Ben and Martinelli were. They had made friends with a guy couple in Beverly Hills when we were in Mexico and went down there for long weekends as often as they could.

Pam and Diane were on a road trip with Evelyn and Mary. After hearing us talk about it, they had decided to go to Carmel for the weekend.

The last I'd seen them, Mike and Greg were sitting on the aft bench holding hands and looking a lot like two teenagers on a date.

Carter had his arm around me. We were making for the ocean past the Golden Gate Bridge. It was a very warm day and, even on the bay, the wind wasn't very chilly. The weather was clear and the water was calm.

Because of the holiday and the good weather, the bay was full of sailboats. It was relaxing to watch them move across the blue water and under the wide orange span of the bridge.

I sighed happily.

"What?" whispered Carter.

"Just loving life."

"It's pretty damn sweet, ain't it?"

I nodded. "It is, at that."

"What do you like best?"

"That's easy," I said. "You."

He squeezed me in close. It felt good.

Author's Note

Thank you for buying and reading this book!

The plot and flow of this story came out of thin air, as with all the Nick & Carter books.

Many thanks, as always, to everyone who has read, reviewed, and emailed me about the Nick & Carter books. It is deeply gratifying in ways that words will never do justice to. Thank you.

Acknowledgments

This is another Nick & Carter story that only briefly leaves the City & County of San Francisco. In order to be able to keep that City of 1954 alive, I've come to rely on the many amazing members of the Facebook group "San Francisco Remembered," for sharing a number of interesting memories and facts that get pulled into these stories, particularly this one. Many thanks for your generosity.

Historical Notes

The events in this book take place between Wednesday, June 16, 1954, and Sunday, July 4, 1954.

The primary characters are all fictional. There are, however, several historical persons and locales portrayed in a fictional manner.

Nick's new office building at 600 Market Street is right in the middle of what is now McKesson Plaza at 1 Post Street. In 1954, the Crocker Building stood at that location. It was an eleven-story building in a flatiron design that was completed in 1891. It was demolished in the late 60s to make way for McKesson Plaza.

On May 9, 1947, the body of Nicholas "Nick" DeJohn, a Chicago mobster who was trying to muscle in on local racketeering and narcotics activity, was found stuffed in the trunk of his car parked at Laguna and Greenwich. Anthony Lima, the head of the San Francisco mob at the time, and his underboss, Michael Abati, along with three other men, were arrested for the murder. The charges were dropped when San Francisco District Attorney Edmund G. "Pat" Brown (who would be elected governor in 1958 and whose son, Jerry Brown, is currently in his fourth term as governor) dismissed the jury and called a mistrial. Brown stated at the time that he didn't believe the primary witness, one Anita Venza. Michael Abati replaced Lima as the head of the crime family in 1953. Abati was deported to Italy in 1961 for being involved in criminal activity and died of natural causes on September 5, 1962.

Johnny DiLuca, Joseph Abati, and "Junior" Abati are completely fictitious persons.

Engraved and custom-designed Peacemaker revolvers (also known as Colt Single Action Army or, simply, Colt .45) were available by special order from Colt's Manufacturing Company. The company employed a number of designers, mostly European immigrants, who became known for their intricate engravings and use of silver, gold, and precious stones in their work.

Silver bullets are pretty but, apparently, lead is more useful (except for werewolves, or so I'm told).

The Old Poodle Dog restaurant has a very long and interesting history. It first opened in 1849. It may not have been the first, but it was certainly the most famous French restaurant in the City. There are several stories about the origin of the name. The first name of the restaurant was *Le Poulet d'Or*. The owner had a pet poodle, considered quite an unusual thing at the time, that was as much of an attraction as the excellent food. Perhaps that, combined with the difficulty of pronouncing the French name, led to the common phrase, "Let's go eat at the Poodle Dog." Whatever the case, this is the name by which the restaurant eventually became known.

The official name changed to "The Old Poodle Dog"

when the restaurant moved to Bush Street in 1868 and then to Eddy Street in 1906. During that time, the restaurant changed owners, expanded its location, and became known as a spot for intimate and discrete trysts in the private dining rooms of its upper floors. It was, in many ways, the epitome of the Gay Nineties. The cuisine was said to be equal to that found in Paris at the turn of the century. Although the business survived the 1906 earthquake and fire, it did not survive Prohibition. The Eddy Street location closed in 1922.

After repeal, Calixte Lalanne, one of the previous owners, opened "Ritz French Restaurant" at 65 Post Street. After he died in 1942, his son, Louis, renamed the spot "Ritz Old Poodle Dog." That location survived until 1980.

"The Old Poodle Dog" was last open briefly in 1984 for about 18 months across the street and inside the Crocker Galleria.

Credits

Yesteryear Font (headings) used with permission under SIL Open Font License, Version 1.1. Copyright © 2011 by Brian J. Bonislawsky DBA Astigmatic (AOETI). All rights reserved.

Gentium Book Basic Font (body text) used with permission under the SIL Open Font License, Version 1.1. Copyright © 2002 by J. Victor Gaultney. All rights reserved.

Sigmar One Font (cover) used with permission under the SIL Open Font License, Version 1.1. Copyright © 2011 by Vernon Adams (vern@newtypography.co.uk). All rights reserved.

More Information

Be the first to know about new releases:

nickwilliamspi.com

Made in the USA
Coppell, TX
28 June 2020